I0555919

Survivors

Forgotten Worlds, Volume 3

Prudence MacLeod

Published by Prudence MacLeod, 2023.

Survivors
(Originally titled Jake)
(second edition)
by
Prudence MacLeod
Copyright 09/2018
All rights reserved.

SURVIVORS

First edition. November 7, 2023.

Copyright © 2023 Prudence MacLeod.

ISBN: 978-1927478196

Written by Prudence MacLeod.

Chapter 1

Shipwrecked

Jake White stifled a groan as he fought the blood from his eyes, desperate to regain his vision. He could hear the great beast that had dragged him here nearby, snarling its defiance at the raging storm outside, the storm that had brought down their ship.

As he lay still, trying to clear his senses, something was poking painfully into his side. It was the big blaster, but the sharp edge pressing into his ribs told him the recoil pad had been lost. He dare not fire it without the pad; it would rip his shoulder off. Alas, he wasn't about to get a choice.

As Jake shifted his weight slightly, a groan of pain was forced past his lips. With lightning speed, the beast turned and leaped at him. Rolling onto his back, he braced the damaged blaster against the stone floor and fired. Those deadly jaws were scant inches away when the point-blank blast hit the creature, hurling it through the cave mouth and out into the night.

With a groan Jake leaned his back against the cave wall. The ground had absorbed the blaster's recoil, saving his punctured shoulder further harm. Shaking off the encroaching darkness, he began to take inventory of his injuries. The beast had hit him from behind and carried him off, leaving a lot of bruises and a couple of puncture wounds. He'd need medical attention, but he could function.

"This a fine mess for a spoiled starship security guy to find himself in, goddamn primitive planets anyway." He continued to mutter against his fate as he cut the sleeve from his tunic and used it to bandage the puncture wound on his upper arm. He was inspecting the wound on his thigh when he heard the low growl from the cave mouth.

"Well, crap!" Jake groaned as he twisted around to brace the blaster for another shot. This wasn't the same animal, but there had been dozens of them. It didn't matter which one it was. As the snarling grew louder the four glowing eyes told him he had two visitors. Aiming the blaster as best he could, he pulled the trigger. Both animals were hurled away, but the mouth of the cave partially collapsed.

The next flash of lightning gave him a clear picture of how precarious the situation was. If he fired the blaster again it would bring the entire hillside down on him. Just as that realization sunk in, he heard the rocks at the cave mouth being pulled aside.

Another groan escaped his lips as he groped for, and found, the projectile weapon on his belt. The blaster fell aside as his other hand grasped the flashlight. Steadying his hands as best he could, Jake flicked on the light and took aim at the crumbled entrance.

"Don't shoot, it's only me." A woman's face appeared in the light, then she wriggled inside and came to him. "Hey, Jake, how's it going?"

"It's been better. Twenty, how did you find me?"

"I could find you anywhere, handsome."

"Stop it, woman, you'll get me killed."

"Jake?"

"You've been flirting with me for weeks, and as much as I enjoy it, I'm married, you're married, and ..."

"I'm SUVI?" She was indeed a SUVI, survivor of unknown viral infection, one of twenty survivors out of six thousand plus humans infected. SUVI; no longer human, but part human and part something else.

"Yes, you're SUVI, but that's a plus, not a minus. Twenty, I'll admit it, you scare the hell out of me."

"Oh?" She continued to poke and prod gently at his injuries, adjusting his bandaging job, plus adding a few of her own from the pack at her side. "I grabbed a first aid kit as I left the ship. There you go, all patched up. So, tell me why I scare you."

"I can't read you. Jeannie has taught me pretty well, and I can read most of the SUVI, but not you, you're different."

She settled down beside him, took the pistol from his hand and fired at the opening. There was a yowl of pain outside then silence. "And that's bad because?"

He sighed, and then groaned as he tried to shift to look into her eyes. "It's bad because I can't read you, I can't tell if you're playing or not. If you are, then all well and good, every guy's ego swells when a gorgeous woman flirts with him, and I'm no different."

"So you think I'm attractive?"

"Stop it, woman, you know damn well I do. If you're not just playing, then I'm well and truly screwed."

"I don't understand. What are you saying here?"

"Twenty, I'm saying if you're serious I doubt I'll be able to resist you, but it'll destroy me utterly. I'll lose Carla, I'll lose the respect of the captain, my friends, all the credibility I've carefully built up with my fellow officers as well as the crew and passengers. Right now, I'm utterly tormented."

To his great surprise she sidled closer and laid her head on his shoulder. "I hadn't thought about any of that, Jake, and I'm sorry for it. Let me tell you a story now. Half of me once had a husband and a good marriage, but that actually ended over thirty years ago; I, personally, never have, and I don't now. Eamon and I decided that too much has changed, and he released me."

"Okay."

"Now, about you and me. You know I'm super intuitive, even more so than Eighteen. Since I first met you, I've known there was something special about you, that you hold something important for me. I guess I started flirting with you to get your attention."

"It worked."

Her sweet rich laughter echoed through the cavern, bringing a sloppy grin to his face. "All right, Jake, I've been set free, but you haven't. So, a little light flirting is all you get."

"Promise?"

"Well, not forever, you're not that handsome."

This time it was his laughter that rang through the cavern, but his cracked ribs changed the laugh into a racking cough. "Oh gods, Jake, I'm sorry."

"Sure you are."

"I am, silly human. Jake, you're a vital part of the Reacher's success and survival. The captain depends on you, and I owe her much. The crew and passengers look to you to keep order. No, no, don't try to deny it. We have something important for each other, you and I, but we'll keep it light and friendly."

He could see the desire as well as the determination in her eyes now and knew that, although she didn't want it this way, she would make it happen and he sighed with relief. "For the greater good?"

"Yes, Jake, for the greater good. So, you do understand SUVI."

"I'm getting there. Now, back to the situation at hand. Put that magic SUVI brain to work and figure out how we're going to get out of here and back to the ship."

"Not to worry, it's getting light out."

"And that's good because?"

"These creatures are nocturnal. With any luck, there won't be a lot of daylighters to contend with."

"What about the storm?"

"It won't let up for a day or two. Hungry?"

"Yeah, I am." He watched in amazement as she pulled a couple of ration bars from the pack at her side. "So, you stopped to pack a picnic before you came looking for me?"

She chuckled at that. "Actually, I packed this bag before we left the Reacher. Something just told me the Explorer would run into trouble.

You were hell bent on going along because things on the Reacher were boring lately."

"That's why you insisted on coming along? Because I did?"

"Because I knew you'd get into trouble, I knew you'd be hurt, but I didn't know the outcome. Yes, I came for you. Happy now?"

"Now I'm really scared." Again, her laughter brought a smile to his face.

THE HISS OF BLASTER fire was lost in the shrieks of the wind that buffeted the small ship. Commander Amanda Drake, her weapon running low on charge, turned to the open hatch, and shouted. "Engineering, report."

"We're all patched up, Commander," replied a voice from inside. "Ship is functional."

The man beside Amanda was using projectile weapons now, moving at impossible speeds as he fought off the attacking predators. "Get back inside, Commander. We need to get out of here."

"No, Thirteen, we've still got people out there."

SUVI 13 dropped another attacking beast as he replied. "We can't help them if we're dead. The ship will soon be blown into that ravine if we don't move. Our people will have to survive on their own until we can come back for them."

He was right, and she knew it. She had to save the rest of her crew and hope against hope those left behind could survive until she returned for them. Against every instinct she had, Amanda Drake turned and leaped back aboard her small spaceship. "Thirteen, get in here and seal her up."

With a leap he was back inside slamming down the hatch. "Hatch sealed."

Even as he spoke the screams of the raging storm outside were muffled, but the sounds of huge claws scraping against the hull were clear. "Three, take her up to low orbit."

"Aye, Commander, bird rising." It was a shaky lift off, and the ship struggled until she rose above the violence of the winds. There was a collective sigh of relief as the flight smoothed out and they escaped the storm.

"Morthel, how many did we leave behind?" Morthel was Earalithian, one of only eleven known to survive, of the trillions in the vast empire they once ruled. Small of stature, with two thumbs on each hand, they were a clever and tenacious people.

The Earalithian woman at the sensor panel looked up with a sad expression. "We left five people on the planet, Commander. Mr. Sacumbtu and two of his men were retrieving one of Lilly's crates. Jake went to defend them as the beasts attacked. One animal carried Jake off, and SUVI 20 went after him. None of these people made it back before the storm hit."

"Where the hell did that storm come from anyway?"

"I have no idea, Commander. It was only showing as gently rising winds on sensors. I warned everyone of the winds, but a moment later it changed horribly."

The small woman was trembling, for in a distant past her colony had been devastated by an event that knocked the planet out of orbit, causing a similar storm. Amanda reached out to gently grip Morthel by the shoulders. "Easy now, girl, easy. This is a different place and time. Look, we're already well out of the storm's way. As soon as it passes, we'll go back for our people."

"I wouldn't advise that, Commander."

"Three?"

"We've patched her up enough to get us home, but I wouldn't take her back into that atmosphere until we've had a chance to make full repairs."

"Can you do that here?"

"No, Commander. We need to get back to the Reacher for that."

"Dammit anyway. Lilly, you on comms?"

"I am, Commander." Lilly Peters, the ship's botanist, looked pale as a ghost, her hands were trembling, but she was holding it together.

"Can you raise any of our people?"

"No."

"The Reacher?"

"I'll try now." She turned away, but the commander's hand fell gently on her shoulder.

"You're doing great, Lilly, hang in there a little longer. Tommy, can you give Lilly something to settle her nerves."

Tommy Mason, the newly assigned medic, handed them each a pill and water container. "I think we all could use one of these right about now." He grinned as he passed them around. "It's gentle, but it will help steady you."

Lilly gave him a weak smile and swallowed the pill before turning back to the communications panel. "Explorer One calling the Reacher, come in Reacher." No reply. "This is Explorer One calling Reacher, Reacher, do you copy?"

The response was faint, but they heard it. "Reacher here, Explorer."

"We've suffered damage and need immediate repairs, Reacher. Are you near?"

"This is the captain; we're still several hours away, can you land safely to await our arrival?"

"Negative, Captain. Ship was storm damaged, barely reached space. We have injured as well."

"Amanda ..."

Commander Drake leaned closer and spoke. "I'm fine, Jeannie, but my poor ship took a pounding, and we had to leave people on the surface."

"We're coming, Mandy, all possible speed. Reacher out."

Amanda sighed and sank into a seat. Her bonded companion, Captain Suvi-jean Sorenson, the former SUVI 5, would waste no time or effort to get to her. "Okay, she's on her way, folks. Tommy, how bad are our injuries?"

"Well, our engineer has a broken arm, so Three took over his job; Alec is in bad shape from a nasty bite. That beast tore him up bad. The rest are bumps, bruises, and sprains."

"I see you're limping."

"That would be the knee sprain I spoke of," he grinned. "Now, how about I take a look at that bump on your head?"

"Sure, why not? Three, can we hold this orbit? Will she hold together?"

"Yes to both questions, but I wouldn't want to try a long jump in her right now."

"Understood. Settle back and rest, people. We'll sit tight and wait for the Reacher to get here. I expect Jeannie will want to send Recovery One down to look for our people. I'd like to be well rested and ready to accompany that rescue mission, same for the rest of you. That's our crew down there and it's our job to get them back."

"Commander."

"Yes, Morthel?"

"I just got a quick look through a gap in the clouds, it was there and gone."

"So, what did you see?"

"SUVI 20 has found Jake, no animals close."

"Now that is good news. Anything on Mr. Sacumbtu?"

"Sorry, Commander. I'll keep trying." Amanda nodded, then with a deep sigh, she leaned back and closer her eyes.

Chapter 2

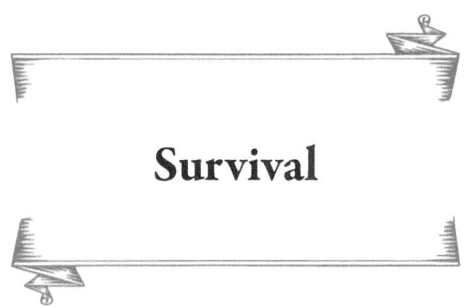

Survival

Jake awoke with a start, disoriented. There was that rattle of stone again. Shaking his head to clear the cobwebs, he managed to focus on the entrance to the cave. The rattle of stone on stone came again. It was SUVI 20 clearing away some of the debris from the entrance.

"Making a bigger hole to let the critters in?"

"No, Jake, I'm making a bigger hole, so I can get you out. You're far too beat up to crawl through the way I got in. I need to open this enough for you to get out before the whole damn thing falls down on us."

Outside the storm still raged with howling winds and driving rain. "Not in a big hurry to go out in that."

She sighed and stopped working for a moment. "I know, me neither, but this place is really unstable. We need to find a better shelter."

"There's another option."

SUVI 20 raised an eyebrow at him. "I'm listening."

"I can feel a cold draft on my back. Maybe this cave comes out someplace else, maybe it has another entrance."

With a liquid grace she moved through the dim light toward him. Stepping past him she stood still, silently searching for the draft. There it was, just a hint of cold air, but she felt it. "Pass me that flashlight." He did.

Twenty flicked on the light and played it over the depths of the cave. She didn't like what she saw. The tunnel narrowed the deeper it went. Reluctantly, she moved deeper into the cave until she had to stoop to go further. "I don't like it, Jake. You're a lot taller than I am and I'm nearly bent double. You'll have to crawl to get this far, and there's no sign of it improving."

"Damn. What does that super SUVI intuition say?"

"It says to go back." Just as she spoke there was a rumble and the cave mouth collapsed. "Jake!"

"Easy girl, I'm all right, but now there's only one choice left."

"We keep going?"

"Afraid so."

"Okay then, we keep going. How are you doing?"

"My leg and shoulder hurt like hell, but I'm functional. This crawling shit is no fun though."

She turned to see him lying prone, using mostly his arms to pull him towards her. "Jake?"

"Leg won't hold me in here, crawling is easier. Keep going now."

With a nod and a look of deep concern she turned back to the tunnel and continued on. It wasn't much longer when they heard the first low growl. "Cover your ears." She wadded something into her own ears then drew her projectile weapon. The sound of it firing could damage their ear drums in that tightly confined space.

Jake quickly put his hands over his ears. She fired three times in rapid succession then moved on. He followed closely, keeping a careful watch on her. Twice more she fired the weapon, then struggled to reload it as they slowly worked their way past the three dead animals.

The tunnel seemed endless to Jake, and his reserves of strength were gone before the cave opened up again. Twenty finished off two more animals then scooted ahead and stood up. Slowly he crawled toward her, tried, and failed, to stand. As he stumbled forward, hands caught him and easily stood him on his feet.

The injured leg failed, and he toppled into her arms. She held him up easily, a grin of mischief on her face. "Why, Jake, I didn't think you cared."

He got the leg under him and managed to stand on his own. "Stop it, woman."

"Okay, I'll stop, but I won't like it." She released him to stand on his own.

He shook his head ruefully as she stepped back, that naughty grin still on her face. "Gods, you're a bad woman."

"Oh come on, you like it."

"Far more than I should, and you know it."

"Yes, I am a bad woman. What are you going to do with me?" The twinkle in her eye brought a great laugh from him. "Stop it. I don't suppose you have anything left to eat in that pack of yours?"

She pulled the bag around from her hip and looked inside, fishing out a ration bar and passing it to him. She took one for herself then turned toward the entrance where the raging storm was easily seen. "That doesn't look friendly."

"No, it sure doesn't. That magic of yours got anything on the ship?"

"They're in orbit, the ship is damaged, more of us are still on the ground but I don't know where."

"Well, crap. There's not a lot we can do to help them in that. I guess we might as well settle down and wait it out."

"We should cuddle to share body heat," she grinned, as he sank to the floor and rested his back against the stone wall.

That brought a bellow of laughter from him. "Come here, you naughty thing, come here and cuddle with me."

Still grinning, she sank to the ground beside him and snuggled up close. Jake put his arm around her and pulled her onto his shoulder. "Behave."

She started to reply, but noticed his gaze focused out the opening into the storm. "They're okay, Jake, at least for now. The worst of the predators seem to be nocturnal, and the rest are waiting out the storm like we are. There's nothing we can do to help our people right now."

"I know. You say the Explorer made it into orbit, but no more. If they were able to contact the Reacher, then help is on the way."

"Yeah, I get the sense they did and you're right, at least I hope so."

Jake suddenly noticed she was trembling and cuddling closer. He started to say something when it hit him, she's SUVI. SUVI have strong group instincts, having been created from a virus endemic to a herd animal. They need to be close to others, be in a group, preferably a group of SUVI.

He put his other arm around her and cuddled her close, resting his cheek on the top of her head. "It's all right, honey, I've got you. We won't be alone for long."

"Jake?"

"You're SUVI, you need others close by to survive. Right now you're the only SUVI on this blasted planet and you're getting twitchy, ready to run out into the storm, desperate to find your own kind."

"Oh my god, you're right, that's exactly what it feels like. This is strong, what am I going to do?"

"Stay cuddled right where you are. We'll be our own little group of Huma-suvis until the ship gets back."

"Huma-suvis?"

"A closed group, one half human, one half SUVI."

"You're a nut, Jake. Thanks." She hugged him tightly for a moment then laid her head back on his shoulder.

He kissed the top of her head again then returned his gaze to the storm outside. *"Better get that ship back here soon, Sister Jeannie, before this poor girl comes unraveled on me. SUVI don't do well alone."*

AMANDA AWAKENED HALFWAY through a sleep cycle, her head pounding. "Damn. I'd better ask Tommy for something to kill this headache." She struggled upright, straightened her uniform then stepped out of her sleeping booth. Three was also awake.

"You got a headache too, Three?"

"Yes. Commander are you short of breath?"

"Yeah, a bit. What's up?"

"We've got an atmosphere leak. Dammit anyway." She hit the alarm then they both began to struggle into enviro suits.

A few deep breaths from the suit's air supply and Amanda felt her headache recede. Everyone else was getting on space suits as well. "Thirteen, can you find the leak from outside the ship?"

"Easy. There'll be an ice trail for me to follow."

He stepped into the airlock and sealed it. He began his inspection, working cautiously, free floating along the side of the ship being careful not to snag his tether line. It took a while, but he found it then sealed it before returning to the interior of the ship. "Leak is sealed, Commander, only one leak found. Coming home."

"Well done, Thirteen. Three, do we have enough air in the tanks to make it?"

"Negative, Commander. I suggest we leave the suits on and hope the Reacher gets here in time."

"If not then we'll have to chance the planet?"

"Yes, Commander. At least we can breathe the air down there."

"Yeah, how's out ammo holding out?"

"Not good, Commander," said Morthel. "We used up most of it just getting the ship repaired and off the ground."

Amanda sighed and leaned back against the wall. "Somebody give me good news."

"Reacher is only three hours away," said Lilly.

"And that's the limit of the air supply in our suits," said SUVI 3.

Thirteen grinned at the Commander and she shook a finger at him. "Don't even say it, Thirteen. Lilly, cut the artificial gravity to one-tenth."

"Commander?"

"Less gravity will make breathing easier. Everybody remain as still as possible until Reacher gets here. I'd rather not go back into that storm with a damaged ship."

"Understood, Commander. Cutting gravity."

"Come on, Jeannie, hurry up. We're cutting this one too close for comfort."

Chapter 3

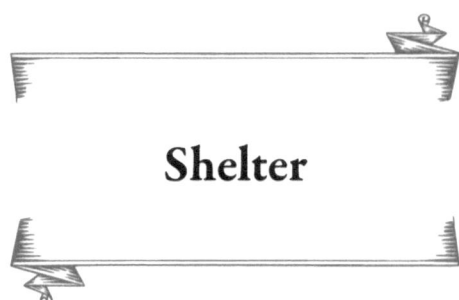

Shelter

Jake drifted between sleep and awareness for hours. The only thing keeping him from giving up to the pain was the woman in his arms. Every once in a while, she tried to snuggle closer, and he could feel the trembling in her body. He suddenly jerked fully awake at the sound of her voice. "Jake?"

"Huh? Yeah, I'm here."

"You sure about that?" A cool hand caressed his forehead. "You're pretty warm."

"It's okay, I'm good. Looks like the storm is easing off a bit. Twenty, am I seeing that right?"

"Seeing what?"

"Over there, is that …?"

"The outline of a shelter, yes, that's no natural formation. The storm's letting up a bit, want to check it out?"

He didn't, but the excitement in her voice caught his attention. She'd stopped trembling and risen to her feet, peering out into the storm eagerly. With a grunt of pain, Jake heaved himself upright. The object of the game now was to keep her mind busy until another SUVI arrived. Limping badly, he followed her out into the rain.

He was soaked through by the time he joined her at the structure. It was built on Earalithian design but was a lot larger. SUVI 20 had already found the entrance and was pulling away fallen debris. Once she had it cleared he spoke in Earalithian. <Door, open.>

With a groan of protest the ancient doorway struggled to open. It made it just enough to let them inside before it jammed. "Since when do you speak Earalithian?"

"I've been working on it for weeks. Seemed like a handy skill to have."

"So, you're always looking for new and useful skills?"

"I have to. I have a SUVI captain to protect, more of them on the ship, and they're all super powered. I'm always looking for ways to improve my skills so I can do a better job. After all, you're the one who told me to keep up."

"I see." She was wandering around the huge room, peering here and there, but there didn't seem to be a lot to the place. "I wonder what this place was used for. Jake, I know you're utterly devoted to the captain. Can you tell me why? What happened for you two to bond the way you have? Don't if it's too personal, I'm just curious."

<Increase ambient temperature ten degrees.> Jake put his back to a wall and slid slowly down as warm air suddenly puffed from several vents in the floor, sending clouds of dust into the room. An exhaust fan began to suck the dust out as he took the weight off his injured leg. "Come here, Twenty, and I'll tell you a story."

"Oh sweet, I love stories." She giggled as she sat beside him and cuddled close. She knew what he was doing, keeping her mind occupied on other things instead of the ache of loneliness and the overpowering urge to run outside in search of others of her kind.

<Door, close.> It slowly shifted back to the closed position. "That should keep the critters off us for a while." He put his arms around her and snuggled her closer, wishing she didn't feel so damn good in his arms.

"It began on the ship, Hermes, said Jake. "My brother and I were born to a pair of hard-core security types, and they raised us to follow that path. The Hermes was ten years out before she dropped off her colonists. We were three years into the return journey when we were told the star where we'd dropped those people off, had gone nova."

"Oh my god, Jake ..."

"Yeah, well, that messed with Mom and Dad more than we knew, but that's a different story. For Hal and me, it was another seven years of training until the ship reached Earth, Earth that was no longer able to sustain life.

"The captain of the Hermes," went on Jake, "the current first officer on the Reacher, Brandon Hoffman, decided to wait for the last two ships to return. Once all five ships were back in orbit, the captains gathered and agreed to blend the crews, rob four of the ships for parts and supplies, then set out to make a colony of their own. They drew straws and Captain Baris of the Reacher won the draw.

"Before the Reacher set sail, the crew positions were awarded, double the actual crew requirements, but they tried to keep everybody busy as possible. When the dust settled there were five security positions up for grabs due to people taking early retirement. Eighty of us applied, they held a lottery, Hal got chosen, I didn't."

Twenty gave him a warm smile. "What happened? You're the captain's go-to guy; how did you get on Security?"

"Patience girl, I'm getting there. I was assigned to Sanitation, working under a bitter chef."

"A chef in Sanitation?"

"Ah-huh. Instead of being the head chef on the Wanderer he was put in charge of Sanitation. We hated each other on sight. Ten years later, when I had finally decided I had no choice, I had to kill him, SUVI 5 came to my rescue. Jeannie was on the Reacher less than two weeks when she got me out of that mess and onto the Security team.

"Commander Hoffman was in charge of Security then, and she'd swiftly become his favorite. He entrusted me with more and more, then when Jeannie became captain it got even better."

Jake smiled as he remembered the euphoria of those days. "Before Suvi-jean became captain, there was an incident where she disappeared for days. We searched the ship, but no sign of her. It was Commander Drake who figured out what to do, and I was the one to make contact. During that time, I called her little sister, and she liked it, we assumed those roles, and I swore to watch her back, to help her in any way I can."

"Wow. That's quite a story," said Twenty. "Thanks for that, and I know what you did."

"What I did?"

"Told me a story, shared a lot of yourself I'll bet you rarely share, and kept my mind off my mad urge to run away, to search for others of my kind."

"Did it work?"

"Better than you might expect, Jake. Thanks for that. Can I ask what happened with your parents? Are they still alive?"

"They are, but they're in bad shape. You see, they were young police officers in a large Earth city, millions of people all around. First, we dropped off ten thousand, and those were killed by a nova, then we got back to find Earth devastated, everybody dead, unable to sustain life. It broke Mom and Dad. They spend most of their time in quarters, watching old vids of a busy and thriving Earth.

"Hal goes to visit them once a week, but not me so much."

She reached for his hand and gave it a gentle squeeze. "Why not, Jake?"

"They've given up, Twenty, completely. They hardly speak when I do, except to answer questions. They trained me most of my young life, and I dreamed of how proud they'd be to see me succeed."

"Not so much?"

"Not even a grunt of approval when I told them I was now a sub-commander and second in command of Security. Dad said it was too easy to succeed when there wasn't any competition, now if I'd made that promotion in one of the old cities, that would be something to celebrate."

"Oh, Jake, I'm so sorry."

"Thanks, but it's okay, I know a lot better than that. There's a lot of Security people of their age aboard the Reacher, with the same skill set and training they had, but I got past them. Suvi-jean Sorenson gave me a chance to prove myself, dug me out of the shithole where I was and gave me a chance. I'll worship her to the day I die for that."

"I happen to know she's pretty fond of you too, big fella. It's too bad about your parents, but I think I can understand how it hit them. I'm from a big Earth city too, and it's hard to really absorb that it's gone. Must have been hell for everybody to see the home planet devastated like that. For me it's not quite real, you know?"

"Yeah, I get that. For us younger folk who were born on the ships it's different. This is all we've ever known."

She sat back and raised an eyebrow at him. "You younger folk?"

"You know what I mean."

"No, I don't really, explain it to me." She tried but couldn't hold back the laughter. "God you're fun to tease, Jake."

"Woman, you'll be the death of me yet."

"You like me," she said, as she snuggled under his arm. She could sense the weakness in him. *"Come on, people, get back down here, the big guy needs a medic."*

"REACHER CALLING EXPLORER, come in Explorer. Still no answer, Captain."

"Keep trying."

"Yes, Captain. Reacher calling Explorer, come in Explorer."

This time he got an answer, but it was faint. "Explorer here, Reacher. What's your ETA?"

"Explorer, this is the captain. We're about an hour away, can you hold?"

"Negative, Captain. This is Lilly Peters, we're all in atmo suits, but the air won't last nearly that long. Commander Drake and SUVI 3 are preparing to take us back into the atmosphere if you can't reach us in time."

"I understand your ship is damaged, will it withstand re-entry to the planet's atmosphere?"

"Amanda here, Jeannie. We have no other option. We expect she'll hold together, but we'll need Recovery to come take us home. We can get on the ground, but she won't rise again under her own power."

"Understood. Can you not wait for us?"

"We lost too much air with that atmo leak, and our suits were already close to depleted. Three of the crew are already unconscious. We're going down, wish us luck."

"Mandy ..." there was no response. "Sensors?"

"The Explorer just went into the atmosphere, Captain. That storm is playing hell with the readings, I've lost her." Jeannie sighed and looked at the Second Officer.

"I'm sorry, Captain, but if we increase our speed we'll over-shoot the planet completely and have to back track."

"Understood, Emmet. Do your best." She reached for her comms. "Commander Volkov, this is the captain. Come to my briefing room, bring your First Officer and Chief of Salvage with you. All senior staff to the briefing room, repeat, all senior staff to the briefing room."

Several calls responded at once. "On our way, Captain."

In a few moments they were gathered at the long table in the Captain's briefing room. "What's going on, Jeannie?" asked her grandfather, the First Officer on the crew of Recovery One.

"Explorer hit trouble on the planet. Apparently, a sudden storm and a mass of huge predators caught them by surprise. They managed to reach orbit but had to leave some people behind on the ground.

We were on our way to rescue her when we lost contact. Once we regained comms with Explorer we learned they'd had an atmosphere leak. They've had to set her back down on the surface.

"Olga, you'll want a number of heavily armed Security with you. Chance, you'll have to get the Explorer strapped to Recovery somehow. Carla, you'll need to send extra medics."

"They've got injured? We're not using transporters for them?"

"Something in the atmosphere is messing with comms and more. I don't want to chance the transporters." Carla Marks, Chief Medical Officer on the Reacher sighed and nodded.

"Also, they had to leave people behind when they escaped to orbit. Finding those people in a heavy storm is a job for the SUVI. I'll lead a team of SUVI in search of our missing people. Brandon, you'll be in charge of the Reacher.

"Get ready, people. I'll meet you at the launch bay."

WHILE JEANNIE WAS CALLING her meeting, SUVI 3 was fighting the shrieking winds as she struggled to find a sheltered landing site for the battered Explorer One. Eventually she found one, an old excavation of some kind, but the built-up rim blocked some of the winds. It was a rough landing, but she got the ship on the ground in one piece.

"Are we down?"

"We're down Commander," replied Three, "air is breathable. Starting the pumps now."

"Get 'em off," said Amanda, as she struggled out of her enviro suit. "Get those helmets off, breathe some fresh air." She sighed as she took a deep breath then slowly released it. With helmets off, her crew relaxed back against the bulkhead, pulling the fresh air deeply into their starving lungs.

"Lilly, can you raise the Reacher?"

"Negative, Commander."

"How about some of the people we left behind?"

"Nope, sorry. I've got nothing on comms."

"Morthel, any idea where we are?"

"Not really, Commander, but we're a long way from where we were before."

"Well, crap. All right let's just sit tight until we get some daylight. Hal, Thirteen, do what you can to get our weapons charged up and ready. Once we can see what we're facing we'll decide what to do next."

They all agreed and settled down to rest as best they could. "Morthel, relax. Let the sensors look after themselves for a while."

"Yes, Commander. We're alone here."

"Alone?"

"No people, and no predators."

"Alone is good right now," sighed Amanda, as she settled back and closed her eyes. The others agreed and followed her example.

Chapter #4

A New Day Dawns

Jake awakened with a start, he was alone and the door to the shelter was open. "Twenty!" He limped to the doorway as fast as he could, but she met him before he got there.

She caught him as he started to topple sideways. "Easy, Jake, easy. I've got you."

"Sorry."

"It's okay. You were afraid I'd gone off the deep end and run away, right?"

"Yeah, that. Sorry, didn't mean to panic on you. Say, you're looking a little better this morning. What's going on?"

"I believe the Explorer crashed back to the planet. I get the sense that everybody's okay, but just knowing there's two more SUVI on the planet has steadied me a bit."

"Wow. So you think they crashed?"

"That or they had to set her back down for some reason. I get the sense no one was hurt so maybe that's what happened."

"Yeah, they could have run out of fuel or something, I guess."

"Or the ship might have been damaged, but not too badly."

"Doesn't matter, I guess. Any idea where they came down?"

"Look at the sun rising over the mountains, isn't it beautiful?"

"Yep, it sure is. That's only the second sunrise I've ever seen. Now, about the Explorer?"

"Other side of those mountains, Jake."

"Well, crap, that takes the fun out of it, but at least the damn rain quit. Twenty, any idea where all the predators went?"

"That way, between us and our people. Come on, the winds aren't that bad now and you can see the herds from that rise."

"The herds?" Jake leaned heavily on her shoulder as he struggled up the short rise. From the top he could see the vast herd of strange looking animals moving steadily down the valley below. Several packs of the big predators could be seen stalking them. "So that's why we had a more peaceful night."

"Looks like it, big fella. Our problem now is, what do we do next?"

"We stay put."

"Jake?"

"I'm in no shape to try getting past that herd and then crossing the mountain range. We're better off to stay here and let our people find us."

"So, you want to camp out for a few days, just you and me."

He chuckled at the merriment in her eyes. "Stop it, woman. Behave."

"All right, I'll be good, but I won't like it. What do we do while we wait?"

"Well, we could mark an old Earth distress signal in that open space right there."

"An S.O.S. made of stones, I love it. As a girl I was always making those in the sand at the park or the winter snow in our backyard. Here, you hold the weapons and keep watch, I'll carry the stones to build the signal."

"I can ..."

"You're wounded, Jake, and I'm SUVI, a lot stronger than you anyway. You be my bodyguard and I'll build us an S.O.S. After that maybe we can find enough dry things to burn, make a smoke signal too.

"Have you figured out what that shelter of ours might be?"

"No idea at all, Twenty. Maybe after you've got the distress signal all set up we can explore a bit."

"Oooh, sounds like fun, sweetie." She was grinning naughtily, and he just shook an admonishing finger at her. With a laugh of mischievous delight, she returned to the task at hand.

The sun was high, and Jake was dozing on his perch. Twenty put the last stone in place and stood up, arms wide, and sang, "Ta-da!" When he didn't respond she spun around to look for him. He was nearly falling from the rock, and she spotted the predator moving on him from behind. "Jake! Look out!"

Years of training kicked in and he threw himself from the stone, turning to land on his back. The sudden move caused the gigantic cat-like creature to miss. With a hissing snarl it spun to leap at him, but it got the full force of the hand blaster and went spinning over backward. As it righted itself he put three bullets into it and it fell over, dead.

SUVI 20 sped past him and, with a scream of challenge and rage, brought a huge stone down on the skull of the second beast, killing it instantly. Jake was just regaining his feet when she came to him, helping him to stand and gathering him into her arms. "Are you okay?"

"I am now."

He was grinning, and she stepped back, her mouth forming a perfect O. Suddenly a bright smile beamed his way. "Why, Jake honey, did you just flirt with me? Oh, gods be good to me, now we're getting somewhere."

His great bellow of laughter brought another smile to her face. "So tell me, big fella, are these things fit to eat, do you think?"

"Eat?"

"We're nearly out of ration bars and have only one bottle of water left each."

"Damn. Okay, they might be. Have you got anything in that pack we could use to light a fire with?"

"No, you got anything?"

"I got nothing. Looks like we're truly screwed."

"Maybe not yet. When I was a girl, I mean when Tara was a girl, she joined the scouts and learned how to make fire, on Earth."

"On Earth?"

"Yeah. I can do it, but I don't see the required materials handy."

"What do you need?"

"Something for tinder, a piece of steel, and a flint. Some of this stone might work, and the butt of that big blaster for steel, but I don't see anything for tinder, and then there's the other."

"The other?"

"For a fire to keep burning it needs fuel. I don't see a lot of fuel around, do you?"

"What do you need for fuel?"

"Seriously?"

"Seriously. I grew up on a spaceship, not a lot of fires around, and if one happened it got put out quickly. On a ship, fire is deadly, not friendly."

"Right, sorry, Jake. I should have realized you youngsters wouldn't have any experience groundside."

"Us youngsters?" He tried to look indignant but failed and her laughter brought a grin to his face. "Okay, girl, looks like we need to go exploring. Let's go see what we can see."

"It appears there are more structures behind the one where we sheltered for the night. Want to check out some of those?"

"Absolutely. With any luck we'll find something to eat that didn't try to eat us first."

She grinned as she led off. "Yeah, well, I'd say it's better to eat than be eaten."

"Amen to that, sweet sister, amen to that." She heard him check the weapons as he limped along behind her.

"THIS IS WHERE THE EXPLORER was, Captain."

"Are you certain?"

"Yes ma'am, these are the right coordinates."

"All right, so they were here, but had to go back down. Calculate the speed of the planet's rotation then extrapolate a likely location for their landing site."

"Captain?"

"Easy, Emmet, I don't expect you to pinpoint their actual location, just a likely spot for us to start looking. Sensors."

"Sensors, aye, Captain."

"Anything?"

"Sorry Captain, nothing yet, but the storm down there seems to be dissipating. With luck we'll be able to get something soon."

"Keep at it, people. Brandon, the ship is yours, I'll be joining the search teams on the Discovery."

"Jeannie?"

"This could easily turn into a hard search on the ground, my friend. A ground search on an unfriendly planet is a job for the SUVI. I'll take Two, Twelve, and Nineteen with me, Thirteen is already on the surface. If it comes to a hard search, the SUVI hunters will lead it."

"Yeah, that makes sense I guess. Good hunting, Captain. Stay in touch."

"I will." She smiled as she lightly slapped his shoulder and fled the bridge.

DOWN IN THE LAUNCH bay, the crew of Discovery was waiting, as were the SUVI. Frank Baris looked and swallowed hard as he saw his granddaughter approaching, dressed in her old hunting leathers. He knew all too well what that could mean, SUVI 5 was ready for battle.

Commander Volkov spotted her and spoke. "Ah, there she is. Are we ready, Captain?"

"Not yet, we're still waiting for the storm to fully abate, and the bridge is working on a likely set of coordinates for us to begin our search. SUVI, are you all prepared for the hunt?"

Nineteen stepped toward her and passed her a weapons belt. It had the standard blaster plus projectile pistol as well as two long bladed knives. "We are, Five. I thought you might want a weapon with a bit more punch. I'm told the predators down there are quite large."

"Thank you, Nineteen, you're quite right. Twelve, is that a scatter blaster?"

"It is, Five. I like the technology."

She grinned at that. "Olga, are your people ready?"

"They are, Captain. Chance Morita has hand-picked the salvage crew for Explorer."

At that point Commander Linsey da Silva and SUVI 18 arrived. "Linsey, why are you here?"

"We just heard what was happening, Captain. Two ships can search a lot of ground faster than one. We can take our ship along to help with the search. Antha is already recruiting a full crew of Earalith."

"It was my thought to leave your ship aboard the Reacher in case of need, but what you say does make more sense. All right, Linsey, get your crew aboard your ship and join us on the hunt. You're right; two ships can cover a lot more ground, and faster, than one."

As they all boarded their ships, the call came from the bridge. "Bridge to Captain Sorenson, we have a set of likely coordinates for your starting point. Transmitting to Recovery One now."

"Thank you, Bridge. Sorenson out."

Jeannie turned to see her Chief of Medical and the Chief of Medical Research approaching. "Carla? Eamon?"

"You'll need medics," replied Carla Marks. "Jake is lost down there and so is Tara- I mean SUVI 20."

Jeannie nodded. "All right then, Carla, you're with Linsey aboard Friendship, Eamon with us on Recovery. Seal them up people, let's get out there."

Within moments the two ships were hanging in space. "That storm needs to calm down a bit more before we can start a search, Captain."

"I know, Olga, I know. I learned my lesson when I tried to rescue Grandfather. I'll just go sit over there with the rest of the SUVI and you can let me know when we're on the ground."

Commander Volkov grinned as Suvi-jean returned to join her companions. She turned to her first officer. "Mr. Baris, anything on comms?"

"Not yet, Commander. I'll keep trying."

"Mr. Morita, anything on sensors?"

"Negative, Commander. Too much interference."

"Keep at it, people, keep at it."

"What the hell does that child think she's doing?"

"Mr. Baris?"

"It's Commander da Silva, she's taking her ship down into the storm."

Suvi-jean was at his side in an instant, grabbing for her comms. "Linsey, this is the captain. What's your plan?"

"da Silva here, Captain. Relax, my Earalith crew assures me the ship is quite capable of handling the storm. They've flown such ships through this type of weather before. I'll see if I can locate Explorer for you. Then I'll ..."

"Linsey, Linsey ... Dammit, lost her. I hope she knows what she's doing."

"And so say all of us," sighed Olga Volkov.

ABOARD HER SHIP, COMMANDER Linsey da Silva shook her head as she realized they'd lost the comm connection. "Ship, are you sure about this?"

"Ship is secure in the ability to navigate through the diminishing storm, Captain da Silva." The ship's AI continued to call Commander da Silva, Captain. It was his little joke.

"Antha, are you getting anything on comms?"

"Not yet, Commander."

"Eighteen, anything on sensors?"

"Nothing on Ship's sensors."

SUVI 18, Commander da Silva's lover, was amazingly intuitive. "What about your SUVI sensors?"

Eighteen chuckled at that. "SUVI 20 is under great stress but managing."

"Which way?"

"I have no idea, Linsey, sorry."

"If we were on the ground, could you get a general direction?"

"Perhaps, but no guarantees."

Linsey sighed then looked to Antha who nodded. "Okay then, Dorind, you're the engineer, can we chance a landing?"

"Oh yes, Commander Linsey. Ship will be fine, no worries."

"Sounds good. Mendalo, keep those guns warmed up. There are big nasty predators down there. We don't want to get eaten."

"Aye, Commander."

"Ettelan, find a likely spot and set us down."

"Aye, Commander Linsey," smiled the small man at the pilot's controls. "Setting down."

Chapter #5

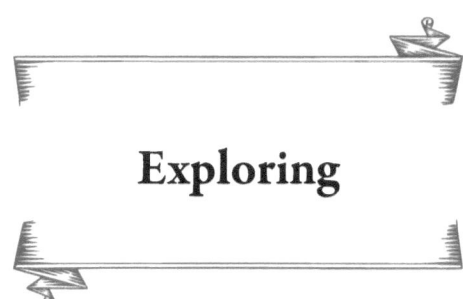

Exploring

Jake and SUVI 20 had been poking around for hours. Tired and hungry, they returned to their original shelter, having gathered some dry wood for a fire. She didn't say, but Twenty doubted they had enough to keep burning for long, or to cook any food. As they reached the shelter, she noticed the animals she'd killed earlier were missing.

"Twenty?"

"Yeah?" She could hear the fatigue in his voice and didn't like it. He'd pushed that injured leg a lot harder than he should have.

"I don't see any dead animals, do you?"

"No. Guess I'll have to go hunting."

"Okay, just remember to come back to me."

Even as he spoke he started to sag toward the ground. She caught his arm and held him up. "I gotcha, Jake. Open the door now, let's get inside where it's safe."

He nodded as he leaned heavily on her arm. <Door, open.> With a scraping sound of protest, the door slid halfway open. Twenty practically carried him inside and settled him down where he could see the entrance. <Door, close.> "It's pretty warm in here, I must have left the heat on."

"Men never think to turn off the lights," she grinned. A cool hand rested lightly on his forehead for a moment. "Not liking this, Jake, you're the heat source. Here, you need to eat." She passed him a ration bar.

Jake chewed slowly for a moment. "You not having one?"

"There's only one left, I'm saving that for you."

"You have to eat too, girl."

"I know, but I'm SUVI, I can last longer without it, and you're injured, you need the food to heal."

"Yeah, I guess. Dammit it anyway." <Bring us food.> Nothing happened.

"What did you say?"

"I told it to bring us food. It was worth a shot; the heat came on when I asked for it."

"Try a few different commands, see what happens."

"Okay, why not?" <Produce food.> Nothing. <Supply nourishment.> This time a voice responded.

<Sleeping quarters only. Food disbursement three buildings south.>

"Holy crap."

"Jake, what did it say?"

"It said the mess hall is three buildings to the south. That must be the big one we didn't find an entrance to."

"Okay, then we settle down for the night and check that out first thing in the morning."

"Bugger that, you need to eat too. We go now."

"Nope. You're exhausted, injured, and there are nocturnal predators out there. We rest until morning, that's an order."

Jake sighed deeply and leaned his back against the wall, closing his eyes. "Yes, ma'am, I hear and obey. First thing in the morning."

SUVI 20 cuddled up to him and supported him as he began to slump sideways. He was already asleep. *"Come on, Captain, get down here. The big guy needs a medic and we're out of food and water."*

Twenty awakened much later to hear him muttering in his sleep. She leaned closer to hear and was able to distinguish a single word. Thirsty. She sighed as she searched her pack and realized she'd already given him the last of the water. Worse yet, she would soon need water herself.

She gently began to shake his shoulder. "Jake, Jake honey, wake up now. We need water. I'll go see if I can find some. I'll be back as soon as I can."

Still groggy, he caught her hand. "No, stay here, stay safe." <Give me water.> Nothing happened so he spoke again. <Water.> There was a groan of ancient machinery, then several basins of some sort appeared from different points on the wall.

Curious, Twenty rose to investigate. Each basin had a handle, so she grabbed one and gave it a twist. There was a faint rumble of machinery from below then, slowly at first but increasing with time, a stream of foul-smelling brackish water began to spout into the air then fall back into the basin.

SUVI 20 held the handle tightly and as the water continued to flow it began to clear. Hesitantly, she first sniffed at it, then tasted it. Delicious. With a cry of delight, she drank her fill then went to retrieve one of the water bottles to fill for Jake. As soon as she released the handle the basin retreated into the wall.

"Shit. Okay, I can do this." She retrieved two empty water containers then approached another of the basins. She turned the handle, and the same process was repeated. "Jake, Jake, come here and drink up then I'll fill both containers for later."

It was a struggle for him to gain his feet, but he made it to the basin where he leaned heavily against the wall and drank greedily. When he'd had enough, Twenty filled both containers and tightened the tops. The basin retreated into the wall. "Feeling better, big guy?"

"Yeah, I am a bit. Okay, that worked, how's our time?"

"It's a couple more hours to daylight, I think. Want to settle back for another nap?"

"Sure, why not?" He returned to his spot against the wall and settled down. Twenty gave him the last ration bar and he chewed thoughtfully. "Twenty, what's your take on our situation, are we getting out of this alive?"

"I don't know, Jake, I just don't know. My intuition isn't telling me anything here, but I still think we'll make it."

"Oh?"

"Yeah. Like I said before, I have this sense you and I are meant to do something special together. We can't do whatever it is if we're dead. Right?"

He chuckled at that then threw the empty ration wrapper across the room. "Yeah, that does make perfect sense. So tell me, if we can't find any food from the old machines, what do we do? I mean, starship kid here, never been hungry in my life and have no real idea where my food comes from."

"Well, the machines did give us water, but if there's no magic food to be had we'll have to do it the hard way."

"Explain the hard way."

"We kill something then cook and eat it."

"What aren't you telling me?"

"Most creatures prefer not to be killed, so they either run away or they fight back. There's a lot of skill involved with primitive hunting that neither of us has."

"But you said you did."

"I was in scouts as a child. I learned to make fire, but I've never hunted, killed, or cooked meat over an open fire."

"Okay, so let's take it one step at a time, first we have to kill something. I have three rounds left for my side arm. One well-placed shot should do the trick."

"Agreed, but as soon as it's dead we have to cut off some of the meat then hurry back here with it."

"Explain."

"Think about it, big guy. The smell of the blood or the sounds of the kill will bring the predators. They'll take it away from us if they can and we're getting dangerously low on ammo."

"Yeah, good point. So, we make a kill, cut off some meat and make it to shelter, then what?"

"We make a fire and put the meat on long sticks and hold it over the fire until it's cooked enough to eat."

"Sounds simple enough. Not that easy?"

"Is it ever?"

"No, girl, it usually isn't. Look, I'm not that sleepy, want to go out hunting?"

"You don't want to try the mess hall first?"

"No, we already looked all over that thing and couldn't find a way in. Besides, this planet looks to have been abandoned for a long time, what are the odds we'd find anything edible?"

Twenty sighed and leaned her back against the wall beside him. "You're right, our odds of survival are better if we can learn to hunt and gather."

"Hunt and gather?"

"That's how our species evolved over millennia, Jake, by eating what they could kill or gather from the land around them. It could take our people a while to find us, if they ever do. We need food now."

"So, we hunt?"

"We hunt. Let's go."

"WE'RE ON THE GROUND, Commander da Silva."

"Thank you, Ettelan. Eighteen honey, are you getting anything?"

"That way, and down. I sense Explorer is that way."

"Okay, good. Antha, anything on comms?"

"Sorry, Commander Linsey, nothing."

"Oh well, that would have been too easy. Ettelan, take us up a bit then proceed along the direction Eighteen indicated."

"Aye, Commander, ship rising. Proceeding."

They travelled slowly, constantly monitoring the sensors and comms. Suddenly Eighteen held up her hand. "Stop, we've gone too far. It's more back that way. I'm sorry, Linsey, I ..."

"Hush now, my love, you have nothing to apologize for. We're trying to get close enough for sensors to pick them up, that's all. We'll follow your keen intuition until it gets us close enough to make contact.

"Pilot, turn us back onto the new direction and proceed slowly."

"Aye, Commander, coming about. Proceeding slowly."

A few minutes later Antha gave a shout. "Stop, I have something on comms.

"Explorer, this is Friendship calling, do you read?"

Eighteen grinned and pointed in a new direction. "Ettelan, just a bit more that way, I think." He nodded, and the ship moved slowly in a new direction.

"Explorer, this is Friendship, do you copy?"

The response was faint, but they heard it. "Linsey, what the heck are you doing down here?"

"Looking for you, Commander," grinned Linsey, as she leaned over Antha's shoulder. "Keep the channel open so we can track you down."

Eighteen had moved to sensors. "Got them, Linsey. They're down in some sort of pit or something. It's pretty deep, but well sheltered, sending location to the pilot's station now. Ettelan, got the coordinates?"

"Got them. Heading down."

Within minutes Friendship had landed beside the damaged Explorer. Linsey, Carla, Antha, and Eighteen spilled out the hatch and hurried to the stricken ship. As they entered there was a cry of delight as Antha hurled herself into Morthel's arms. "Oh my love, when I heard there were injured I was frantic."

"Easy, sweet Antha, easy. Yes we have injured, but I'm not one of them."

Amanda grinned as Linsey appeared through the hatch. "Good to see you, Linsey."

"Good to see you in one piece, Commander. I had a quick look. Your poor ship took a pounding all right. How about I give you and your crew a lift back to Reacher. We can send the ship's location to Recovery, and they'll pick her up for a ride back to the repair bay."

"Works for me."

"Mandy, where's Jake?" asked Carla, as she frantically looked all around.

Amanda took the distraught woman in her arms. "I'm so sorry, Carla. Jake was attacked and carried off by an animal. SUVI 20 went after them, and we learned from sensors she'd found him and driven off the predator. We then lost contact."

"SUVI 20? She's with Jake?"

"Yes, is that a bad thing?"

"Depends on how you look at it. Ah well, if anyone can keep him alive it'll be a SUVI. Let's get these folks back to Reacher where I can tend to them properly. Tommy, help me here."

"Yes, ma'am." With the strong helping the injured they soon had all aboard Friendship.

Amanda stood gazing all around. "Wow, Linsey, I didn't realize there was so much room in your ship."

"Yeah, Ship was originally a scout ship carrying troops, then he was refitted as a shuttle on the colony. Thing is, he's still got all the tough working parts of a scout ship. That's why we could venture into the storm where Recovery couldn't.

"Mendalo, is everybody aboard?"

"All are aboard, and the ship is sealed for transport, Commander."

"Awesome. Ettelan, take us home to the Reacher. Antha, as soon as we can contact Recovery, send them the coordinates for Explorer."

The ship rose easily into the air then shot toward open space. There was a moment of sway as they hit the open winds, but then smoothed out as they rose above the storm. "Commander da Silva, I have Recovery for you."

"Thank you, Antha. Well done. Recovery, this is Friendship, do you have the coordinates for Explorer?"

"Coordinates received, Friendship. Good job. What are your plans now?"

"We have the crew of Explorer aboard and are heading back to Reacher with the injured. We'll drop them off then return to join you in the search for the missing crew members."

"Linsey, this is the captain. Is Amanda aboard with you?"

"Right here, Jeannie."

"Are you all right, my love?"

"I'm in one piece, don't worry. I'll be returning with Linsey when she comes."

"Wonderful news. Is Thirteen injured?"

"I, too, am in one piece, Five. I will return with the ship to assist in the search."

"Excellent. I have Two, Twelve, and Nineteen with me as well. The SUVI hunters will be the main search party on the ground."

"Understood."

"We'll be back as quick as we can, Captain," said Linsey. "Friendship out."

The small ship hurtled past the orbiting Recovery and straight to the Reacher where the launch bay doors were waiting open. As soon as those doors closed, and atmosphere returned to the area, the ship was swarmed by medics with Carla shouting orders.

Once the medics had the area cleared, Linsey stood by the hatch of her ship. "All right, folks, we're headed back down. Who's coming along?" Jake's brother Hal, SUVI 13, Amanda, and Morthel hurried aboard.

"That's everybody? All right, Mendalo, seal him up. Ettelan, take us back to the place we left Recovery."

"Aye, Commander da Silva, launching now."

In short order they were back orbiting beside Recovery. "This is Friendship calling Recovery."

"Go ahead, Friendship."

"I understand that you have a SUVI search team aboard. How about you transport them over here, then I can focus on search and rescue while you focus on salvaging the Explorer?"

"This is the captain. I like it, Linsey. Make room, we're coming over."

A few moments of time and a flash of light brought the SUVI search team aboard Friendship. "Welcome aboard, Captain."

"Thank you, Linsey," smiled Jeannie, as she hugged Amanda tightly. "What happened down there?"

Amanda sighed as she stepped back. "We landed easily after two days of flying a full search pattern. We'd spotted what we thought might be a former settlement of some kind, but once on the ground we saw no real evidence of it.

"Morthel was on sensors and warned us the winds were picking up. I called for everybody to return to the ship, but we were suddenly attacked by packs of predators. Mr. Sacumbtu and two others were cut off. Jake started toward them when an animal hit him from behind and dragged him away.

"Thirteen tried to recover him but was overwhelmed by beasts and had to retreat to the ship. All that happened in an instant, but in the same instant the storm dropped down on us, and the winds flipped the ship over a couple of times. SUVI 3 got it righted and we all retreated to safety.

"We made it back into space and called you, but developed an atmosphere leak before you could get to us. We had to set her down again."

"What about Jake?"

"SUVI 20 was with us, and she took off after him. While Thirteen fought the predators, she slipped by them and disappeared into the storm. When we were lifting off again, Morthel caught a glimpse with the sensors. Twenty had found Jake and got him free of the animals, but that was two days ago. We have no idea how they're doing now, or if they're even alive."

"Eighteen?"

"I believe they're still alive, Captain, but I have no idea where."

"Thirteen?"

"I expect we'll find them, Five, but alive or not, I can't say."

"All right then, since Ship will stand up to the storm, take us down to where Explorer was when it all went to hell."

"Sorry Captain, but we have no idea where that was. The coordinates for that location might be in the computer of Explorer, but we don't have them."

"Dammit. Eighteen?"

"Sorry, Five, no idea. A long way from Explorer's current location, but that's all I can say."

"All right, take us back to Explorer, let's see if we can find those coordinates."

"Aye, Captain, going down."

As Friendship neared Explorer again, Antha spoke up from sensors. "I've got a dozen or more life forms at the Explorer's location. All animal, none human or SUVI."

"Looks like you're up, Mandalo," grinned Linsey.

"Aye, aye, Commander. Manning the weapons. Make a slow pass over the area, Ettelan."

"Slow pass, aye," came the reply.

The small Earalithian began to work the weapons controls feverishly. "Pass complete," said the pilot.

"Four life forms still active."

"Four still alive, aye. Another pass if you please, Ettelan," grinned the gunner.

The pilot obligingly turned the ship around and made another pass. Again, Mandalo worked the guns. "No active life forms, Captain," said Antha, not looking up from her sensor screen.

"Set us down close, Pilot."

"Close it is, Commander da Silva." There was a soft bump, and they were on the ground.

Once aboard the Explorer Morthel called up the sensor memory. "I can only get a partial set of coordinates, Captain. The original damage taken when we flipped over must have shaken things up a bit. I can put us close to where we were, but that's it. Sending coordinates to Friendship now."

"Back to the ship, now." Startled, they all turned to Linsey who'd sounded the alarm. "Now, hurry."

She was running and, not sure why, the rest began to follow her. Once outside the early morning light showed the massive landslide moving towards them. "Get in, get in." Linsey stood beside the hatch waving people on, urging them to hurry.

As the last one boarded she leaped inside and slammed the hatch down. "Ettelan, get us in the air, now." Linsey wavered a bit on her way to the captain's chair as the ship beneath her leaped skyward.

"Danger averted, ship is clear," said Eighteen. She was staring at the sensor consol. "Commander Drake, I fear your ship is lost."

"What???"

"That landslide buried her deep under tons of sloppy storm-soaked mud and soil. It'll be a mighty task to dig her out again."

Amanda Drake sank slowly into a seat, her face ashen. "Gone, and without Linsey's warning, so would we be."

"Easy, sweet Mandy, we'll get her back or build you a new and better one."

"Thank you, Jeannie, but right now we have people lost on that planet. We need to focus on rescuing them, or discovering their fate if we can't. I know that goes against your SUVI instincts, but we're human, they're human, and one of them is SUVI ..."

"Easy, sweetheart, easy. We'll do as you say. We need to reclaim our people before we think about anything else. Linsey, get me Recovery."

"Aye, Captain. "Recovery, this is Friendship calling. Please acknowledge."

"Recovery here, Friendship. Olga Volkov commanding."

"Olga, it's the captain. Our medic returned to Reacher with the injured. Since we'll be the search team, can you send over one of yours?"

"Eamon's on his way, Captain." The Chief of Medical Research for the Reacher arrived in a flash of light.

"Oh, Olga, we were on the ground with Explorer when a landslide buried her deep. We just made it out in time. Look it over and decide if you want to try a retrieval or to pass on it as too dangerous. I'll leave that decision to you."

"Thank you, Captain. That storm seems to be clearing now; we'll go down closer and take a look. Recovery out."

"Okay, Linsey, this is your ship, do what you can to find us a starting point."

"Aye, Captain. Ettelan, what have you got?"

"Not much, Commander. I've got enough to start a grid search, but not much more."

"Do what you can, Ettelan."

Several hours of careful search later they'd found nothing. "Ettlan, why have we stopped?"

"Those mountains ahead, Commander Linsey. The line I'm following from Explorer's records runs right through them. Were they in the mountains?"

"No, we were on more open country," said Amanda.

"So the question now is, which side of the mountains, this side or the other? Direction, Commander Linsey?"

"Antha, we turned up anything on sensors yet?"

"No, Linsey, not a hint."

"Dorind, you get anything on comms?"

"Not a squeak, Commander."

"All right then, probably not on this side of the mountains. Ettelan, take us over the hills to the other side and we'll start again."

"Aye, Commander." The ship rose gracefully and flew across the wide mountain range. It was growing dark on this side as they arrived. The pilot brought the ship down close to the ground and proceeded along the search line.

"Comms?"

"Nothing yet, Commander."

"Sensors?"

"I'm getting a reading, something small, but metallic dead ahead."

"What is it?"

"Unknown, Commander."

"Ettelan, put us down beside it."

"Aye Commander. Object located, setting down."

They alit cautiously, spilling a heavily armed SUVI team out onto the ground first. When the others reached the ground Dorind nodded as he inspected the metal object. "It's the aft buffer panel from the Explorer, no question. Looks like we're in the right neighborhood."

"Maybe," replied Amanda. "Those were powerful winds, that panel could have been blown halfway across a continent by now."

"Perhaps not," mused Suvi-jean. "We were following along the line provided by Explorer, and we found the panel right on the line. I think we're on the right track. Thirteen?"

"Makes sense to me, Five. We should continue to follow the line, sweeping carefully with sensors."

He barely finished speaking when Suvi-jean drew her weapon and fired. There was a yowl of pain from a huge cat-like creature as it began to thrash about. They fled back into the ship and swiftly lifted off.

"These things are a lot more active at night," sighed Thirteen.

"Then take us up beyond their reach and we'll rest until the light returns. There's little we can do in the dark anyway."

"Ettelan, take us up."

"Aye, Commander Linsey, going up. Low orbit established over coordinates of the found buffer panel."

"Well done, Ettelan. Folks, there are sleeping quarters back here, but they're sized for Earalith, could be a bit cramped."

"Thank you, Linsey, we'll manage," sighed Suvi-jean. "Get some rest people, we'll start again in the morning."

Chapter #6

Learning to Hunt

The presence of the large predators had kept Jake and SUVI 20 inside until well after dawn, but eventually they made their way outside. Nothing within sight moved, so they set out toward the south. A careful search still didn't find them an entry point into the mess hall, so they continued on.

Suddenly, Twenty threw out her arm to stop him; she'd spotted a lizard of some sort. She patted Jake's arm and pointed out the creature. It took a few moments for him to spot it as it blended in with its surroundings. Jake nodded then took careful aim. A single shot rang out, the lizard twitched once, kicking its feet, then lay still.

Twenty ran to it, pulling a small knife from her pack. "What are you doing?"

"You have to remove the entrails from the kill," she said as she worked. "At least, that's my understanding of it. This animal is small enough for us to carry back to the shelter. If it were larger we'd just take a piece of it and go."

She rose to her feet, holding the carcass out at arm's length and shaking it to get all the offal out before setting out for the shelter. Jake followed closely, wary for danger. They were nearly back to safety when they heard the yowl of a hunting beast behind them. The predators had found where they'd made their kill.

<Door open!> shouted Jake as they hurried along. With a groan of protest the ancient door complied and was waiting for them. They hurriedly pushed inside. <Door close.>

Twenty dropped her prize onto the floor and sank to the ground, resting her back against the wall. Jake slowly eased himself down beside her. "So now what?"

"I've brought meat, now you cook it for me." She tried to keep a poker face, but the look of surprised indignation he gave her made her giggle. "God, you're so much fun to tease."

Jake chuckled and shook his head. "Woman, you're heartless. Stop tormenting me and tell me what's the next step."

"Now we make a fire and cook the meat. We have those two long sticks, so the rest of what we have can go for firewood. You cut off some strips of meat and I'll try to get a fire started. Make sure you peel all the skin off it."

Looking somewhat dubious, Jake took out the knife from his belt and reached for the dead lizard. The back legs looked to have the most meat on them, so he began there. Twenty gathered the dry leaves and small twigs they'd gathered into a pile, keeping the larger sticks aside.

Jake watched carefully as she brought the driest of the leaves into a tiny pile then held the exposed butt of the blaster over it and banged it with a stone several times. Nothing happened, so she inspected the stone carefully then tossed it aside. She picked out three more just like it and discarded them as well.

Selecting a different type of stone, she tried again. Another failure, and more discarded stones later she got lucky on her third try, a small spark flew through the air to land on her tinder, but it instantly went out. A few tries later she got a good spark. Cupping her hands around the live spark, she blew gently onto it and was rewarded with a small flame.

Grinning with delight, Twenty carefully fed the small dry twigs to the flame until she had a reasonable fire going. Jake now had two strips of meat skewered on the long sticks. She reached for one then held it over the fire. "Like this, Jake. The meat will change color as it cooks."

He nodded and held his piece over the fire, mimicking what she was doing.

Twenty threw the rest of their fuel onto the small blaze. "We need more heat to cook this right, I just hope it lasts long enough."

As the flames rose a bit higher there was a rumble deep beneath them. "What was that?"

"Don't know, Jake, but I've got a bad feeling about this."

"Keep the weapons close."

Nothing more happened for several moments, then they heard a soft hiss. Jake turned the meat he was cooking then sniffed at it. It smelled good and he was ravenous, then he heard a second hiss above them. "Ah for fuck sake, you're kidding me. Dammit it all to hell. Come on, Twenty, let's move."

He surged to his feet, clutching his portion of meat as he hurried toward the exit. <Door open.> "Come on, Twenty, hurry."

"Jake, what the ..." She suddenly shrieked as foul-smelling water began to drip down on her. She grabbed her pack, and, clutching her cooked meat close, raced for the door. Outside, sputtering and swearing, she shook the muck from her hair and eyes. "What the actual hell?"

"Sprinkler system."

"You're kidding me."

"Nope. I guess our little fire triggered it. Meat seems to be cooked though."

He was grinning at her, and she started to laugh. She tasted the meat and nodded. "Not bad. Not bad at all for our first attempt at hunting."

Jake took a bite and nodded his approval also. "Yep, I agree, it tastes okay. Next time let's make the fire out in the open and sleep inside where it's dry."

"Yeah, good plan, but it's soaking wet in there right now. We need to find a new shelter for tonight."

Jake took another bite of the meat and sighed. "Yeah, that truly sucks. The critters will be moving around soon, how about our old cave for the night then we find something better in the morning."

"Works for me, big fella. Eat up now and we'll get on the go."

It was growing dark as they entered the cave, it was empty. With full bellies and plenty of water, they settled down for the night. Twenty snuggled close and Jake put his arms around her, cuddling her close. *"Damn, she feels so good in my arms. It's just not right. Got to get a grip on this."*

Deep in the night his bladder awakened him. He gently untangled himself from her embrace and stood up. "Jake? Jake, are you okay?"

"Easy girl, nature calls, that's all. I'll be right back."

"Promise?"

"I swear it. Stay there, stay warm."

"Okay, you be careful."

"I will." He moved to the mouth of the cave and looked all around. Nothing moved in the light of the two moons, so he stepped out and to the side, unzipping his pants. As he relieved himself something penetrated his awareness. He no longer ached to hold Twenty in his arms. "What the hell?"

He was still puzzling that over as he returned. She looked up to smile at him and pat the ground beside her. *"This is seriously weird shit,"* he thought as he sank down beside her and reached to pull her close. She felt so perfect in his arms.

Twenty purred and snuggled deeper into his embrace then went back to sleep. Jake didn't. He lay awake, his mind racing even as he rested his cheek against her hair. "Okay, Jakob my old son, as Thirteen would say, use your brain. Something strange is going on here.

"When I'm close I just want to hold her tight, but ten yards away and not so badly. Give me a bit of space and it eases up somewhat, let me get close, see her smile at me and all bets are off. Why? How does that work? Think Jake, think.

"Okay, this sweetheart is SUVI, each SUVI is different, they all have superpowers, but all are different. Twenty is so intuitive it's scary, bet she has some sort of super SUVI sex appeal too. Okay, so now we know what the danger is, the trick will be to walk that edge without falling over. I don't want to hurt her, I don't, but I dare not give in to the attraction."

He lightly kissed her hair and held her gently then finally drifted off to sleep again. He was jerked awake to her battle scream. Jake leaped to his feet, weapons at the ready, to see her standing over a dead animal, a bloody stone the size of his head in her hand. "Hi, Jake, sorry to wake you."

"Wake me? Looks like you kept me from being eaten alive, that makes it okay." Her laughter brought a grin to his face.

"It's not daylight yet, you settle back down, it's my turn for a potty break." With that she slipped out the cave mouth, leaving him alone with the dead beast.

"She's out of sight and I'm fine again. Hmm." He was leaning back against the cave wall, chewing thoughtfully on a piece of last night's meat when she returned. Jake patted the ground beside him, and she sat then cuddled close. "Twenty, tell me a story."

"Tell you a story?"

"Yeah, I told you my sad story yesterday, your turn now. Tell me all about yourself."

"The other SUVI left the planet and you could see that, couldn't you? All right, a story it is, Jake.

"Long, long ago, on a planet far, far away, a girl child was born to a young couple who could ill afford to have children. Tara Louise Carstairs grew up hard, on the fringe of a large but very dangerous city. There were few luxuries, the two summers in scouts being the highlight of her childhood. She managed to survive into adulthood, in spite of the world she lived in."

"Oh?"

"Her parents died of a plague thought long gone from Earth, but people who couldn't afford the vaccines began to get sick. Tara's parents died, she didn't. By the time she was eighteen she was working two jobs, trying to get herself into a better neighborhood, move up out of the bad side of town, when she met a medical student named Eamon Reilly.

"Eamon was a genius, and accustomed to getting everything he wanted. He wanted Tara and, through him, she saw her way out of the crushing poverty. They married and for the next four years Tara worked three jobs to keep them alive while he finished school and rocketed to the top of his field.

"She had less than a year in the luxury apartment he managed to get for her, less than a single year of being the lady of leisure she'd always dreamed of becoming."

"What happened?"

"The disease that took her parents had lain dormant in her body, but finally bloomed, and it resisted all attempts to cure it. After enduring months of severe pain, dozens of Eamon's attempts to heal her, Tara gave up and asked for the suicide drink. She was tired of the pain, the weakness, and just wanted to be free of it all.

"Eamon, as we all know, tricked Tara and put her into cryo sleep, waiting for the day he would find the cure. He failed. Tara thought she'd endured pain before, but it was nothing compared to what happened then. In the arms of a group of SUVI, Tara Reilly died in pain, and SUVI Twenty was born.

"When the captain told her she was unique, the first to be able to explore herself, to become who or whatever she was to become, unfettered by the need to work to stay alive, she rejoiced and swore to do just that, to give herself that freedom every child should have, that she never did.

"That's what I do now, embrace each day and try to discover whatever joy it might hold."

"Mmm, so that's why you pick on me, you're having fun."

She laughed at that and gave him a gentle squeeze. "You are fun to tease, Jake, never doubt that. Look, I'm sorry if I've caused you any distress. I've never actually felt this strongly about anyone before."

"Not even Eamon?"

"No, he had the hots for me, and I saw a path to a better life. He was gentle with me; I did everything in my power to make him happy he'd chosen me, and I came to love him dearly. That was very different.

"The way I feel about you is new to me, I guess I just gave in and enjoyed it, never thinking about the cost to you. I'm truly sorry, Jake. Nothing has changed, but we'll stay hands off."

"For the greater good?"

"Yeah, for the greater good. You know, I always believed that if everyone shared equally in everything, it would be a much better life for everybody. I guess I lucked out, I woke up on a spaceship where it works like that, no rich people, no poor people, everybody shares equally. I like this, and I'll do everything in my power to protect it, even to pushing down my feelings for you."

"Twenty ..."

"Easy, Jake. Look, you already have one SUVI sister, can you deal with another?"

"I'm doing pretty good so far." She chuckled at that and gently elbowed him in the ribs.

ABOARD THE FRIENDSHIP, Suvi-jean and Amanda cuddled in the small bunk. "Mmm, this is cozy."

"Yes, it certainly is, are you comfortable, Mandy my love?"

"Huh? Oh sure, I'm fine. Just snuggle down here on my shoulder."

Suvi-jean settled down, but still felt the tension in her companion. "Mandy, what is it?"

"Huh? What is what?"

"Sweetheart, I can hear your wheels turning from here. What's on your mind?"

"Oh, I'm worried about the folks we had to leave behind, I guess."

"I understand, but there's more, isn't there?"

"Yeah, there is. When Friendship arrived to rescue us, Carla was with them. She asked what happened to Jake. I told her an animal had carried him off, but SUVI 20 had found and rescued him."

"So?"

"She looked angry at that news. You'd think she'd be happy he was all right; she sure didn't like the idea of Twenty being out there alone with him."

"Okay, what am I missing here?"

"Honey, remember how you felt when you saw Lathan kiss me?"

"Yes. Oh. Oh dear, has Jake been taking an interest in Twenty?"

"Actually, Twenty's been flirting shamelessly with Jake. I think she scares him."

"Scares him?"

"Yeah. I think he likes it that she does it, and that scares him."

"I think I'm still missing something here."

"Sweetheart, if he likes Twenty flirting and Carla finds out, she'll be hurt. If he really likes Twenty, either Carla or himself will be hurt. If he doesn't like it then Twenty will be hurt. At this point it appears that Carla has noticed the flirting, and now, no matter what Jake does, somebody's going to get hurt."

Suvi-jean sighed deeply. "Now my head hurts. This is one of those human complex situations that nobody fully understands, right?"

"Absolutely right, my love."

"Humans are strange creatures."

Amanda chuckled at that. "You like us, Suvi-jean, you know you do."

"Yeah, I do, sweetheart. I just hope they're both all right and staying safe."

Chapter #7

Staying Alive

While Amanda tried to sooth Jeannie to sleep, Jake too, was having trouble sleeping. SUVI 20 lay snuggled up to him, sleeping soundly, but sleep eluded him. *"Boy, this is some mess I'm in. This would have been so much easier if this gal was just a teenager with her first crush, and in a way that's just what she is, but she's not really. This woman is a hard-nosed survivor.*

"So, where does that leave me? On shaky ground, that's where it leaves me. Come on, Jeannie, get back here and get us out of this mess. I need a medic and I need to see Carla.

"Ah hell, first things first, we need to survive."

He was still ruminating a while later when she began to stir. She stretched and yawned, then lightly kissed his cheek and rose to her feet with a dancer's grace. He caught his breath and looked away. When he looked back she was grinning at him. "Like what you see, big fella?"

Jake struggled to his feet then sighed. He pulled her close and kissed the top of her head. "You know I do, too damn much. Now behave, we have to hunt and gather."

With a laugh she danced out of his arms and out of the cave into the morning sunlight. Jake shouted a warning as the beast pounced.

Twenty's SUVI reflexes saved her as she dropped to the ground and rolled back to her feet, causing the beast to miss. As it turned to snarl at her Jake saw the cute girl vanish and the hardened survivor appear in her answering snarl. She had come to her feet with a large stone in her hand. As the predator tensed for another charge, her arm flashed forward.

The stone struck the beast in the head, crushing its skull. It lurched, twitched, then fell dead. Twenty seized the creature in her hands, swept it into the air then smashed it against a boulder. A final kick for the corpse then she turned back toward Jake, shook herself slightly to release the mood then beamed him her brightest smile. "Look, Jake, meat."

"Woman, you truly scare me sometimes." He limped toward her as he spoke. "I thought you were a goner."

"In the ghetto where Tara grew up there were packs of feral dogs. She learned early to carry rocks and how to throw them accurately. That skill saved her more than once. Gotta admit though, I'm way better at it now."

She looked closer and saw the distress on his face. Stepping into his arms she hugged him gently. "Easy, Jake, easy. I'm okay. You get some meat off this critter while I see if I can find enough fuel to get a decent fire to cook on."

He nodded as she walked away toward the mess hall they'd been unable to gain entry to. Focusing on his work, Jake was unaware of impending danger until the huge predator roared a challenge. Looking up Jake saw something new, almost lizard like, three times the size of the cat creature he was cutting on.

The beast roared again then charged. Jake fled as fast as his wounded leg would carry him. He ran away from the direction Twenty had taken. It was almost on him when he heard the smack and the beast yelp. He glanced over his shoulder to see it change direction, going after SUVI 20.

She threw another stone that smacked the animal on the head then she ran. "Noooo!" Jake turned to follow, but the ground disappeared from under him, and his shout of protest turned into a scream as he fell into the darkness below. He hit the bottom hard and lost consciousness.

Up in the daylight, the monstrous animal was still pursuing SUVI 20. She had no idea what had happened to Jake, but she ran on until she was certain she'd led the beast far enough away. Once sure, she poured on the speed, dodging around rocks, behind ancient buildings, and open caves.

As soon as she was certain she'd shaken off the pursuit, she returned to the last place she'd seen Jake. He was nowhere to be found. She located his footprints in the sandy dirt, then followed them to the edge of the hole in the ground. It was dark inside; she couldn't see the bottom.

Twenty called and called but got no answer from below. Her near panic was broken by the sounds of the monster coming in her direction. "Screw it, if Jake's down there, then I'm going down." She stepped into the hole and vanished just as the beast reached for her.

It was a long drop, but her SUVI muscles absorbed the landing. She called out for Jake but got no answer. Slowly, carefully, she began to feel her way around, searching for a wall or some other guide. The floor sloped downward, and with her hand lightly resting on the wall for guidance, she set out, stopping every few paces to call out for Jake, still no answer.

Eventually she gave up and sank to the ground, heart wrenching sobs shaking her slender frame. She'd lost him. Somewhere down here was the man she loved beyond reason, and she'd lost him. She didn't even know if he'd survived the fall. In the utter darkness of the underground tunnel, SUVI 20 cried herself to sleep.

WHILE TWENTY SLOWLY succumbed to the sorrow and the need for rest, Jake gave in to the pain that insisted he wake up. It took a few tries, but he got his eyes open and managed to heave himself around to take the pressure off his aching shoulder. "Dammit, I'm in bad shape here. I almost wish I had a shot of Commander Hoffman's whiskey, probably do me good right about now.

"Okay, super security guy, do this right. First take stock of the injuries." Painfully he moved his limbs and flexed his muscles. "All right, everything still works, shoulder feels like it's on fire, and my back is aching, the wound on the leg seems to be healing a bit, so that's good. Ribs feel like they're cracked, deep breathing hurts. That's not so good."

"All right, standing up now." He managed to get to his feet, but immediately fell. His right knee wouldn't hold him. "Well crap, must have twisted the knee when I hit the ground." He squirmed around until he had his back braced against the wall. "Now, body's in bad shape, but still functional. Now for the rest."

His exploring fingers located his weapons. He checked them as best he could. One shot left in the pistol, low charge on the hand blaster, and the big scatter blaster was completely drained. Cursing, he threw it aside. "No sense dragging that around now, it's broken and useless."

Further exploration of his resources gave him more bad news. The meat he'd saved was gone and the water container had been damaged in the fall. There was only a small trickle left in it. Jake swallowed every drop he could squeeze out then cast the damaged container aside, listening to it clatter along the floor to disappear into the darkness.

His belt still contained the long-bladed knife and the flashlight. A quick flick of the light showed it to be low on charge as well. He shut it off to save the charge for when it might be most needed.

"All right, should get moving, staying here won't do any good." His shoulders moved as he tried to get to his feet, but that was all. "Crap," he muttered as he closed his eyes and melted back against the wall. He was instantly asleep once again.

Jake awakened several hours later; he was moving slowly. It took him a moment to understand what was happening, something had hold of his boot and was dragging him along. He groped for and found the gun and the flashlight. Flicking the light on he saw a lizard like creature gripping his foot in its mouth.

He fired the last bullet and the creature fell dead as did the flashlight. Jake kicked the dead creature off his foot, an act which used the last of his reserves. With a groan he lay back and closed his eyes again.

SUVI 20 AWAKENED WITH a start, that had been a shot. Jake! Where had it come from, which way? She shouted but got no reply. "God dammit, Tara, use that SUVI brain and work this out. You're a superwoman now, the man you love is down here in the dark, hurt and under attack. Use your brain and find him.

"Okay, Jake's hurt, and he was before we came down here. It was a long fall for me, it would have been a lot worse for him as he was already in bad shape. So, where is he? Probably back near where we fell through. Which way is that? Think, Tara, think.

"Wait, I came here by following the wall with my left hand touching it. If I put my right hand on it, I should be able to get back to where I started." She surged to her feet and set out, stopping to call his name every few paces. She got no answer.

Eventually Twenty arrived back near the starting point, she could not only see the stars out through the hole they'd fallen through, but hear the shrieking winds rising as well. Once again she called out for him. "Jake?"

It was faint, but she heard the groan nearby. "Jake, talk to me, make a sound so I can find you." She listened with all her might and finally heard it, a faint tapping sound. Moving in what she hoped would be the right direction, she listened. The tapping came again three taps, three harder and three more quick taps. It was the SOS signal she'd taught him.

"I'm coming, Jake, just a little more ..." she'd seen it, the faint dying glow from the flashlight. She leaped to his side and gathered him into her arms, tears streaming down her face as she cradled his head against her breast. "Jake, oh god, Jake. I thought I'd lost you."

He sighed and relaxed into her arms. It felt so good to be held by this alien woman, this super SUVI. He gave her a gentle squeeze then croaked out a word. "Water."

"Water, yes, I have water. Here, love, easy now. Sip it slowly." She carefully gave him all she had.

The water seemed to revive him a bit. <Light.>

"Easy Jake, easy honey. You've got a big goose egg on your noggin. Take it easy." She kissed his forehead and hugged him to her again.

Jake sighed with contentment. Surely it was no betrayal of anybody or anything just to enjoy a moment of this. Finally he roused himself a bit and repeated the word. <Light.>

Tears filled her eyes again as she held him. "Aw Jake, please focus. Please honey. That's Earalith and I can't understand what you need."

"Repeat the word," he murmured softly from her shoulder.

"What? Repeat the word? Why? Never mind, say it again so I can get it."

<Light.>

She tried. <Loogie.>

Jake tried to laugh, but only managed a chuckle and a cough. "Try it again, Sweetie."

"Why Jake, did you just call me sweetie?"

"Oh sure, take advantage of a guy when he's weak."

She chuckled and cuddled him closer again, kissing his forehead. "You know it buddy, I've got you now. Okay, give me that word again."

<Light.>

This time she got it. <Light.>

"Louder."

<Light.> she shouted. Nothing happened for a moment, then they heard it, a steady tick ticktick. Far away they saw two lines of lights coming on, moving closer to their position. They watched as the lights marched past and on up the hill.

The tunnel was now bathed in light, and she could see the shape he was in. "Oh god, Jake."

"Easy now, sweet sister, easy. I shot the meat, now you have to cook it."

"What? Why you big ... Oh Jake, you're so hurt. I ..."

"Easy now sweetie, easy. Haul me back so I can sit up against the wall. Have you got anything left for ammo?"

"I've got three in the gun and a small charge in the hand blaster."

"Okay, you're deadly with the pistol, leave me the blaster and go exploring. We need food and water, or whatever you can find. If nothing, then we need a way out."

"No, I'm not leaving you again, ever."

"Twenty, honey, I'm all beat up, and unless you want to watch me eat that bugger raw, you'll have to go exploring."

"Eat the bugger raw? Gross."

He chuckled at that. "Go on, girl. You're in good shape, you'll be able to cover a lot more ground without me."

"I don't want to be without you, Jake. I don't."

"Twenty ..."

"Okay, but you stay right there, I won't be long." With that she gently braced him against the wall, kissed his forehead then sprinted away, going downhill. She soon disappeared around a slight bend.

Jake watched her go, that ache for her still strong within him. He was aware as it faded, but only slightly. She'd been crying as she found him, held him, and he hadn't felt so safe and protected since he was a child in his mother's arms. "Well, crap, this just sucks. Okay, face the truth and deal with it, Jake.

"The truth? This is no teenage crush; this girl has a real thing for you. The whole truth? I'm developing a real thing for her too. So, what do I do now? Give in to it? I can't, I just can't. I can't do that to Carla. I love her, and I can't do that to her. Twenty? She's SUVI, she'll push it down for the greater good. Now I have to suck it up and do the same.

"Sometimes life is just no damn fun at all." He put his ruminations aside, SUVI Twenty was on her way back.

"This place is some kind of a mining operation, or it was. Nothing useful down that way, checking the other way now. Are you okay?"

"I'm good, girl. You go explore."

"Be right back." She patted his shoulder and trotted away, heading uphill.

Chapter #8

On the Hunt

Suvi-jean sat bolt upright as she felt the ship move. Both she and Amanda scrambled into their clothes and hurried out to the small bridge. Linsey was already in the captain's chair with SUVI 18 beside her on sensors. "Linsey, what's up?"

"I know it's early, Captain, but there is a bit of light down there. We have to get moving, there's another big storm forming up south of where we need to search. If it moves as fast as the last one we won't have a lot of time."

"Understood. Get us down there as fast as you can. SUVI, prepare."

As they checked their weapons and pulled on the heavy safety jackets, Jeannie noticed Amanda gearing up as well. "Sweet Mandy, no. You can't come with us."

"I have to. Those are my people down there, I have to ..."

"You have to let us find them, sweetheart. We SUVI can move faster, survive longer, and have hunting experience far beyond your abilities. Please, Mandy, stay here with Linsey, get everything organized for the retrieval of injured. If they're not, then so much the better, but I fear we will be facing injured people when we find them."

"She's right, Commander Drake," said Antha, as she relieved Eighteen on sensors. "The surface of that planet is no place for a human or Earalith. With a storm coming this is a job for the SUVI."

With a sigh of resignation, Amanda reached out to gently squeeze her friend's arm. "You're right, Antha. As much as I wish it wasn't, it is a job for the SUVI." Reluctantly, she removed the survival jacket, emptied the large pockets of the ration bars, water containers, etc. She hung it back in the locker along with the weapons belt. "Fine, I'll just sit here and fret."

Morthel gave Suvi-jean a knowing look and spoke. "Actually, Commander Drake, if you could join me at the forward screen, perhaps you might recognize something that would help us, something I might miss."

"All right, Morthel, that's a good plan. At least I can feel useful."

The SUVI gathered by the hatch while Amanda and Morthel focused on the screen, searching for something, anything familiar. The ship swept down to where they'd found the buffer panel, then proceeded along the original line of search. "There, ahead and to the left, near that tall boulder. That's where we originally landed."

Linsey grinned and winked at Amanda. "Thank you, Commander Drake. Ettlan, set us down beside that boulder."

"Setting down ... ship has landed."

He was still speaking as the hatch flew open and the SUVI leaped out. A large animal popped its head up and instantly fell dead. Thirteen patted his weapon and grinned. "That way, Five. The beast carried him off that way and she followed."

The SUVI set out on the search, and Amanda sighed. Again Linsey winked at her. "They're so intense, aren't they? Let's try this our way. Antha, got anything on sensors?"

"Just the SUVI and several animals. Nothing more, Commander."

"Morthel, give the comms a try, see if you can raise anybody."

The small woman smiled and stepped to another station. "This is Friendship calling the crew of the Explorer. Can anyone hear me? This is Friendship calling the crew of Explorer, can anyone hear me?" She got no response except a strange beeping sound. "Commander?"

"That's a comm unit with a drained power source. Can you pinpoint its location? It has to be nearby."

"Got it."

"Inform the captain, please."

"At once, Commander. This is Morthel calling Captain Sorenson. Come in please."

"Sorenson here."

"Captain, we've located a drained comm unit about thirty meters ahead and to your right."

"That's great work, Morthel." As if controlled by a single mind the SUVI swept to their right and moved ahead. "Sorenson to Morthel, where?"

"About two meters dead ahead of you, Captain."

"Understood."

Jeannie and the others stood gazing at the pile of rubble. "It must be under that."

"Or beyond it, Five," said Eighteen. "I think that hill is hollow."

"Let's find out," said Nineteen as he began to lift away some of the heavier stones.

They all pitched in and soon had the cave entrance somewhat uncovered. Eighteen, being the smallest, wriggled through and turned on her light. "I have the comm unit, Five, but there's no one here. Searching for a back entrance now."

"Wait for me, Eighteen," called Jeannie, as she and Thirteen crawled into the cave. "There could be more predators here and we wouldn't want anything to happen to you. Linsey would abandon us here if we let that happen."

Eighteen chuckled at that. "The comm was right here. It's damaged, but it was Jake's."

"There's plenty of animal sign here," said Thirteen, "but here's where he crawled away. Those are a woman's tracks, so Twenty was with him. They went this way."

They followed the tunnel until they found the others entrance. After careful inspection, Jeannie sighed and straightened up. "They were here, then they left but returned, then left again, and recently."

Further scouting brought them to the hut where they'd tried to cook the meat. "Looks like they're out of food," said Thirteen. "They made a kill then brought it in here to cook it."

"Why would they try to cook it in here? The place is soaked and damp."

"Not certain, Captain, perhaps easier to defend, but they're gone from here now."

She nodded. "It looks like they left here in a hurry. The fire area is soaked as well. I'll bet they triggered some ancient fire suppression system and had to flee. That probably drove them back to the cave, but where did they go from there?"

Just then her comm unit pinged. "Jeannie, it's Amanda. Those winds are picking up fast. We're coming to get you."

"Understood. Come to my comm signal."

The winds were strong, and they had to lean into them to reach the ship that landed nearby. "Get in, get in," shouted Amanda as she held the hatch open. Jeannie was the last through then Amanda slammed down the hatch. "Hatch sealed, Commander da Silva."

"Acknowledged. Ettelan, get us above that damned storm."

"Aye, Commander. Ship rising." They felt the ship fighting the fierce winds as it rose through the atmosphere. Finally it smoothed out. "Low orbit achieved, Commander."

"Thank you Ettelan, well done. Captain Sorenson, we've retrieved Mr. Sacumbtu and company, shall we return them to Reacher?"

"You have them? Where?"

"Back here, Jeannie," said Eamon Reilly as he poked his head through a door. "They're in rough shape, but they'll recover. I'd really like to take them back to the Reacher."

"There's nothing we can do down there right now anyway," sighed the captain. "All right Linsey, take us home."

"Aye, Captain, heading home. Ettelan?"

"Heading home, aye."

Jeannie leaned on the back of the captain's chair and sighed. "Linsey, I have to say, you and your crew are amazing. How did you find Mr. Sacumbtu?"

"Same way we found the other comm, Captain. Theirs was drained too, but we located the dead signal."

"Dead signal?"

"Every comm unit has a dead signal, you know, that annoying beep it makes when you need to change or charge the power source. Friendship's sensors are strong enough to pick that up. We found them in a small cave, the mouth of it covered in dead animal bodies. They'd managed to find a defensible position and waited for rescue."

"Well done, Linsey, all of you. I can see a greater role for you and this amazing ship in the near future."

"Actually, Captain, it's Ship and crew that deserve the praise, I just sit here and take up space."

"That is untrue, Captain da Silva," came the voice of the ship's AI. "Each crew is only as good as the captain who leads them. You are intelligent and decisive as any captain I have encountered before."

"Ship is correct, Commander Linsey," agreed Dorind. "We the crew are more than happy to have you in the captain's chair." There were murmurs of agreement from the other Earalith.

"So be it," said Jeannie, as the ship settled into the launch bay of the Reacher. "Everybody catch a rest period then be ready to set out again at the first sign of that storm abating."

As they disembarked from the Earalithian scout ship, Jeannie reached for her comm. "All senior staff to the bridge, repeat, all senior staff to the bridge."

Amanda linked her arm through Jeannie's as they strode along. "Sweetheart, what's going through that busy brain of yours now?"

"Just something that needs to be done for the good of all, Captain Drake."

"Ah-huh, wait, what did you just call me?"

"You heard it right."

"Jeannie, what are you thinking."

"Patience, my love, I'll explain all as soon as everyone gets here."

They entered the briefing room to find most of the staff already there. As soon as all were gathered, Jeannie rose to speak, her eyes glowing amber. "People, some time ago I was chosen to be captain, to be the one leader, and you all agreed this was what you wanted.

"I have done my best, and, in all modesty, I believe I have succeeded. However, the learning curve has been steep, and one thing I learned the hard way is, you can only captain one ship at a time.

"When Recovery One got in trouble I went running off to save Grandfather, but it was Commander Drake who reached past my panic, gently took back command of her crew and efficiently made the rescue. That lesson was reinforced this past day as I watched Linsey guide her crew to a far more successful rescue mission that I managed.

"My point is this, I would like to change a few things here. The Reacher is the mother ship, nurturing and holding our combined species safe. It is my task to captain her, and I rejoice in that.

"However, now we have smaller ships that work independently of the Reacher, and yet report to her. I'd like to promote each commander of our smaller, yet vital ships, to the rank of captain. I believe they've all earned it."

The first officer then spoke up. "Captain, I have no objection here, but can you clarify a bit more about how that would all work?"

"Of course, Brandon. Amanda, for instance would retain her position on the Reacher, as would all her crew, but once aboard the Explorer she would be in command, just as I am on the Reacher. It would be the same for all the smaller ships and their commanders.

"So, opinions people?"

Brandon Hoffman chuckled. "Well, since we're becoming a fleet, in a way, it does make sense, but there's only one problem."

"And that is?"

He grinned at her as he spoke. "With a bunch of new captains running around, you'll have to assume the title of admiral."

"What???"

"He's right," agreed Olga Volkov. "If you don't want the title it will only lead to mass confusion, mutiny, opposing..."

"Oh stop." Jeannie sighed and sank back into her chair. "Mandy, help me here. What do I do?"

"I like your idea, Suvi-jean, but Commander Hoffman's right. It will work well, but you'll have to become Admiral Sorenson."

"Now wait, I've been doing a bit of research, and if I assume that title then I have to appoint a new captain for the Reacher."

"Don't want to lose your job?"

Jeannie sputtered then burst out laughing. "No, I like my job, I want to keep it."

"Can I offer an alternative?"

"Please do, Commander Drake, by all means, help me here."

"We the commanders of the satellite ships remain Commanders while on the Reacher, then assume Captain's rank aboard our own ships. In essence we'd be holding dual rank."

"Won't that get confusing?"

"Yes, it could. Maybe it's better to leave this as it is for now."

"I suppose. It's just that I wanted some way to recognize the success of the people entrusted with the new ships."

Linsey gave her a gentle smile. "Forgive me, Captain, but your obvious approval is all the recognition we need." Suvi-jean returned Linsey's smile and allowed her eyes to return to green.

Amanda spoke the question on everybody's mind. "Jeannie, what's going on here? What's driving this for you?"

"Saw through me as usual, didn't you? All right, I'll talk. As captain, everybody looks to me for direction, to have all the answers. The problem is, I don't always have the answers. When Grandfather was in trouble it was you who had the answers.

"Earlier today as I went running off like a primitive savage trying to track our missing people. It was Linsey and her crew who first put me on the right track, then went and rescued several of our missing people.

"The point is, I don't have all the answers, and once off the Reacher I seem to get lost all too easily."

"So that's it," chuckled Brandon Hoffman. "Jeannie, at no point in time did any of us expect you to have all the answers. However, I would point out that one of your greatest strengths is your ability to step back and let someone else take charge when you see the need."

He grinned and leaned his elbows on the table. "Now, the title of admiral doesn't mean you have to give up command of the Reacher. As the flagship of our ragged little fleet, she would naturally be the admiral's ship and the admiral would certainly retain control. There's no need to relinquish your command."

Suvi-jean sat gazing all around the table at the faces smiling back at her. "Do it, Jeannie."

"Mandy?"

"Go on, do it. Nothing will change except the titles, you'll still be our leader, we'll still be in command of our ships, but it will give the crews and the passengers the sense we're getting things done."

"Oh yeah? So what happens next year when we need to put on a show?"

"Easy," grinned Linsey, "then we make you the empress."

Suvi-jean burst out laughing. "Shut up, Linsey. Shut up or I'll make you admiral. All right, consider it done. Captain Volkov, what news of our poor Explorer?"

"Well, Admiral," a grin flashed across Olga's face before she got down to business, "I'm sorry to report Explorer is lost to us. She's too far below all that sludge, we can't even get close to her."

"I see. Moira, can you build us a better version of Explorer, using elements of Earalithian designs?"

"Well, we can, but it'll take some time, and we'll probably use up all the Earalithian metals we have to do it."

"I see. What about that ore hauler we salvaged? Is it ready yet?"

"We're ready to make a few test flights, but I wouldn't want to take her down into that atmosphere. A storm that strong would tear her apart."

"Oh? Linsey's ship stood up to it rather well."

"Friendship was originally a scout ship, Admiral," said Linsey. "He was built tough and weaponized as well as armored. As I understand it, you designed and built Explorer primarily as an escape vehicle."

"Yes, that is true. All right, Moira, consult with Amanda and anyone else she wants to bring in, then build us an explorer that's as tough or tougher than Friendship. Oh, by the way, the sensors on Friendship seem to be a lot more sensitive than ours. See if you can talk Dorind into sharing a bit of that tech, would you?"

"Aye, Admiral. I'll get started on the designs today."

"Excellent. Now, Carla, report."

"We've got everybody patched up, Jeannie. We're extremely lucky no one was killed or more badly injured. Mr. Sacumbtu and his crew are a bit malnourished and dehydrated, but they'll be fine. Can I ask what the plan is to retrieve Jake?"

"As soon as that damn storm has abated enough for us to function, I plan to take the SUVI back to the surface and find him. We'll work from the ground, Captain da Silva and crew will conduct the search from the air."

"I want to come with you."

"That's Linsey's decision. It's her ship, she'll decide who she takes with her."

"You're welcome aboard Friendship, Commander Marks," smiled Linsey. "Captain Drake, you and any member of your crew that you want with you are welcome as well."

"I'll come, Linsey, and I'll bring Morthel, but I get the feeling the rest of us might just be in the way."

"What about Tara, I mean Twenty?" asked Eamon Reilly.

"She and Jake are together as far as we know from the signs we found, Eamon. It looks as though Jake was limping badly, so it's safe to assume he's injured, but she's not. They hunted and made a kill, so we assume they're out of food, but they have managed to sustain themselves."

"You mean Tara has," he sighed.

Suvi-jean leaned back in her chair. "Eamon, please understand, SUVI 20 is as important to me, to this ship, as anyone else. She is utterly unique, and I have great hopes for the wonders she will bring to us.

"Having said that, what should we know about Tara Reilly that will affect this situation?"

Eamon let his head drop into his hands for a moment then sat up straighter. "She's a survivor, Jeannie. Tara grew up in the slums of an old Earth city. She'd managed to work her way up out of there when I met her.

"I was utterly smitten at first glance, but she wasn't. However, she saw in me a path to a better life, and so she married me. Oh, I knew, but to her credit, she was a loving and faithful wife, and I believe she came to love me deeply.

"Anyway, before we met, when she was young, she fought off feral dog packs, rape gangs, and worse. Somehow her parents managed a couple of summers in scouts for her, and there she learned a few basic survival skills that will serve her well right now.

"She can make fire, kill and cook food, perhaps more, and now she's SUVI fast and strong. If Jake White is injured, he's got a lot better chances of survival with her there. As far as I know, he grew up on a ship, has never been hungry, has no idea where his food comes from, etc. Tara will keep him alive if anyone can."

"That is good to know," said Suvi-jean, her gaze fixed on Carla, who never once looked up from her hands.

"Brandon, anything worthy of note going on aboard the Reacher?"

"Nothing has come to my attention, Admiral. Sheila?"

Commander Sheila Singh, Chief of Security, sighed and shrugged her shoulders. "Nothing at all from a security standpoint, Admiral. All quiet aboard the Reacher."

"Now that's a welcome piece of good news. All right, people. Let's get back to it. All personnel bound for the surface of the planet, get some rest. I want to be back there as soon as possible."

Chapter #8

A Turn for the Better

J ake sat braced against the wall, dozing fitfully. Twenty had been gone a long time and he was starting to worry when she suddenly reappeared. She raced to his side and pressed something to his lips. Water. Blessed water, she'd managed to find another source. Jake drank greedily for a moment.

Twenty set the empty container aside then cradled him in her arms and lightly kissed his forehead. "How're you doing, Jake?"

"I've been better."

"I know, honey, I know. Do you think you can walk if I help, or should I carry you?"

"Carry me? Dammit woman, I'll walk, leave me a bit of dignity, can't you?" With that he heaved himself to his feet, stumbled sideways and caught himself against the wall. He sighed and shook his head as she giggled.

In spite of himself and the pain, he had to grin. "Stop it, woman. It's cruel to mock the infirm. Come over here and cuddle under my arm so I can lean on you."

"Oooh, now we're getting somewhere."

"Behave."

"Yes, dear." She put her arm around him to steady him as he leaned heavily on her and took a few steps. *"Oh gods, he's so hurt. Oh Jake, I just have to get you to the end of the tunnel. Please god, let him make it to the end of the tunnel."*

To Twenty's great surprise and delight, Jake slowly began to get his legs under him. "Hey, you're doing better."

"Yeah, danged sprained knee seems to be remembering what it's supposed to do."

"I'm just going to hang onto you, so you don't fall."

"Ah-huh."

She leaned away and gave him a look of surprise, then she noticed the tiny grin on his face. "Oh, now, my big boy is feeling better." She snuggled back under his arm again. "We've got a fair way to go yet, but there's a wonderful surprise waiting for you at the end."

"Sounds good."

She didn't like the sound of his voice and glanced up at him. His teeth were gritted and his eyes unfocused. He was fighting through a lot of pain, but he was staying on his feet. "Stay with me, Jake, stay with me. We're almost there."

"With you all the way, girl."

"I wish." She was expecting to be told to behave again, but instead he melted toward the floor. "Oh, bugger your male dignity." She easily scooped his unconscious body into her arms and carried him the rest of the way.

Jake came to in a stark, yet clean room, lying on a hard bed. As he tried to move, he discovered he was nearly naked, and his wounds were bandaged. He sat up, wavered a bit, then got his balance. Testing his muscles, he found he could move more easily. He was bruised in a number of places, but he could move. With a groan he tried to struggle into his pants.

"Aw, darn, do you have to put them back on?"

"Dammit, Twenty, behave yourself." Her sweet laughter brought a smile to his face. "Did you enjoy getting me out of my clothes?"

"Sure did, Handsome, but it would have been a lot more fun if you'd been awake to help me."

Jake just chuckled at her naughty grin. "About that, how did I get here, and where is here?"

"I carried you after you passed out, and as near as I can guess, this is an infirmary. That mess hall we tried to get into is across the hall. I managed to bring your kill back here and figured out how to work some of the kitchen appliances, at least enough to cook the meat.

"Another one tried to steal the kill, so I cooked the both of them, hungry?"

"Yeah, I sure am. You've got me all stitched up and bandaged."

"I was married to a super surgeon, remember. I learned a few tricks. I found some alcohol and bandages and stuff, then got you all put back together while you were asleep."

Jake slid off the bed and stuffed his feet into his boots. She helped him into his shirt and jacket. "Twenty, I ..."

"Don't say it, Jake. There's no need to say it. I thought I'd lost you and ..." Tears filled her eyes and she hugged him tightly. "Oh, Jake ..."

"Easy, honey, easy." He held her gently and kissed her hair. A huge hand brushed the hair back from her forehead then warm lips touched her skin. "Come on now, you promised to feed me."

She laughed and sniffed at the same time as she gently stepped out of his arms. "Gods, you're such a guy. All right then, soup's on, let's go."

Twenty led him back out into the tunnel then across to another door. Inside there was a huge mess hall. "Kitchen's back this way." Jake followed her into another area where he could smell the cooked meat. He was suddenly ravenous.

"Veggies too? Where did you get these?"

"From the freezer compartments. I figured it was worth a try, this being a mess hall. They're tough chewing, and not much taste to them, but they're food. The meat's quite good.

"Hey, go easy there, big boy. We've been without food for a while now. Eat too much and you'll get really sick. Go easy, there's plenty more for later."

Reluctantly, he pushed away the oversized platter, nodding his acquiescence. He had no idea of what she was talking about, but he trusted her judgement. "Twenty, that was awesome, a feast fit for a starving man."

Again, her laughter brought a smile to his face. "Yep, the way to a man's heart is through his stomach all right. So, now you're all patched up, fed, and rested. Want to do some more exploring?"

"Yeah, we need to find weapons now. There are lizards in that tunnel and one of them tried to eat me. We need weapons."

"We'll have to improvise on that score. This looks like an old mining operation. Maybe we can find some tools we can convert. Jake, we've got enough food for several days now, and access to water. We have time to rest and let you recover."

"Yes, but we also need to find a way to let folks up topside know where we are. I lost my comm unit somewhere, how's yours?"

"Dead. I guess we need to find a way to charge it up."

"We can charge it up in sunlight, but there's none of that here and I doubt we can find a power source connection that will work."

"You never know, maybe I can hot wire it."

"Hot wire it?"

"You know, pop the back off it and off something else then connect them."

"We could try that, but it could fry it for good. Maybe if we find where I fell through there will be enough sunlight to charge it."

"Maybe, but not today."

"Oh?"

"There's another big storm up there, not a lot of light getting through, and I think it's almost dark again."

"How long was I out?"

"Quite a while, honey. You had me scared."

"Yeah, sorry about that."

He rose to his feet then started to topple sideways. In a flash she was beside him, steadying him. "Easy there, big guy, easy. I've got you patched up a bit, but you need to take it easy for a few days."

"Okay, Doc, you're probably right about that. Well then, let's dig in for a while, what have we got left for weapons?"

"Sorry, honey, I've got nothing left."

"I thought you had three shots left."

"I used them up on your dinner."

"What a woman, she hunts, and she cooks. Okay, we need to find some form of defensive weaponry. For now, all we have is the hand blaster. Can we barricade ourselves in here?"

"Tough to do. It'll be easier to block ourselves up in the infirmary. You know, smaller room, one door, stuff like that."

Jake grinned at her. "Yeah, stuff like that. Okay, let's go. So tell me, have you any idea who was doing the mining? I mean, everything seems a bit big for me, no way in hell it was the Earalith."

"Actually, I think it was, but I think they were using slave labor."

"What makes you say that?"

"Those doors up top responded to Earalith, so did the lights down here, yet as you say, everything is oversized. Also, I found something somewhat disturbing."

"Talk to me Twenty."

"The critter you killed, and the one I killed for dinner, have a lot of features in common with a skeleton I found. I also found some charts. Wild guess, the Old Earalith Empire was using augmented lizards to do the mining. When they abandoned the place the slaves were left behind where they devolved back into the original form."

"Well that's just sick and twisted."

"Yes it is, but I've gotten to know a few of the Earalith on the Reacher. They're good people, I just don't see them doing anything like that."

"Me either, but then, remember, our guys were the rebels against the empire. Who knows what sort of shenanigans the empire was up to."

"Yeah, I guess." She looked thoughtful as she sat in the tall chair, swinging her legs like a child. Suddenly she noticed him grinning at her. "Jake White, if you're laughing at me because my feet don't reach the floor, you're in big trouble."

"Oh no, girl, I wouldn't think of ..."

He got no further as he burst out laughing at the face she made, sticking her tongue out at him. She hopped off the chair with a bright smile and gave him a gentle hug. "It's good to hear you laughing, sweetie. Come on now, we'll go back to the infirmary and get you stretched out on that bed again. You need to rest."

He leaned more heavily on her than he would have liked, but he was tired again. She helped him onto the bed then covered him with a blanket. God only knew where she'd found that. She located some sort of control device on the wall and began poking at it until the lights dimmed. She then pulled up a chair beside the bed.

"Twenty?"

"Hush now, sweetie. I'll take the blaster and keep watch; you get some rest." She kissed his cheek, took the hand blaster from his belt then sat beside him.

As his breathing deepened, she turned her gaze from the door to his sleeping form. *Well, Tara, this is a new and interesting turn of events. When you thought you'd lost him it tore the heart out of you. That's new, and we didn't like it. So how the hell are we going to let him go when we get back to the Reacher?*

"Who knows, who cares, right now he's mine and I have to protect him. We'll worry about the rest later." Just then her reverie was broken when he moaned in his sleep. "Easy Jake, easy, I gotcha," she whispered softly, as she lightly kissed his cheek and held him until he relaxed again.

Jake awakened many hours later to find her asleep in the chair, her head resting against the edge of the bed. He stretched, then tested each muscle group. "Yep, still beat up and sore as hell, but I think I'm functional again." He eased himself out of the bed and stepped into his boots.

SUVI 20 murmured but didn't awaken. He smiled at her then gently lifted her onto the bed and covered her with the blanket. A kiss for her forehead then he was out the door, searching for the facilities.

His body was rebelling at all the food he'd eaten. On the bright side, his knee felt much better, and he was barely limping.

A quick search turned up what he sought just off the mess hall. A short while later he was back in the infirmary, sitting in the chair beside the bed. He didn't notice the small grin playing at Twenty's lips. She'd been aware as he laid her on the bed and covered her up, and she'd thrilled at that kiss on the forehead.

A short while later she yawned and sat up. With a smile that nearly melted his iron resolve, she hopped off the bed and stepped to the door. "Potty break. Meet you in the kitchen?"

"Are you cooking?" Her delighted laughter brought a smile to his face as she danced away.

Jake rose and did some poking around before heading back to the mess hall. He had a couple of strange instruments tucked in his belt. Twenty was already there, warming up some of the previous night's leftovers.

She glanced at his new toys and arched an eyebrow at him. "They're really sharp and pointy, as well as made of good steel."

"Weapons?"

"A good start."

"Hungry?"

"Sure am."

"For what?"

His eyes snapped up to see her naughty grin. "Oh no you don't, SUVI 20, I'm not that revived. Behave."

"All right, if I have to, but I don't have to like it. Eat up now, you need your strength."

Again he noticed the tiny grin playing at her lips. "Stop it woman, you're killing me."

To his great surprise she stepped close and hugged him tightly. "I'm sorry, Jake, I just can't seem to stop teasing you, trying to hold your attention. I'll try harder."

"Oh yeah, harder to what, tease me?"

She laughed and gave him another gentle squeeze. "Dang, the man's got me figured out already." A quick kiss for his cheek then she stepped away. "So, what's the plan for today?"

"First, I guess we should find out if it actually is daytime. If it is, maybe we can get a small charge into that comm unit of yours."

"Sounds good. I guess we're going back to find the hole in the roof, right?"

"Right. Twenty, on the way here I noticed a couple of doors to the side. Did you investigate any of them?"

"I tried, but I couldn't get any of them to open."

"Yeah? How did you get the infirmary and mess hall open?"

"They must have functional sensors or something. They opened when I stood in front of them. We can go try a few of those other doors now that you're back in action."

The first door they opened was only a janitorial closet. Jake was all too familiar with those sorts of tools. He chose a long-handled mop and broke off the head. He now had a walking stick that could double as a quarterstaff. The next one they tried was some sort of office, nothing of great use there.

On the third try they found a short corridor to a vast storage area. It was filled with sheets of metal. "Wow, I'll bet Chief Engineer Duncan would love to get her hands on this cache," mused Jake. "There's probably enough metal here to build two or three more Explorers."

"Well, the hulls for sure, but what about the inner workings, you know electronics, computers, things for heating and water systems, stuff like that."

Jake chuckled. "Yeah, they'd need some stuff like that. Should we see if we can find any?"

"Sure, why not?"

They wandered around the storage area for a while but found only stacks and more stacks of metal. Finally, SUVI 20 called a halt. "Okay, it's time for you to take me home, big guy. You're starting to fade on me."

"Yeah, you're right, Twenty. Can you remember the way?"

"Sure, handsome. Stick with me, I won't lead you astray."

"Ah-huh."

She laughed and hugged his arm. "Jake, honey, I do the teasing, remember? If you want me to behave, then don't even start."

"I am duly warned. Hey there, girl, I felt that little tremble. What's wrong?"

She sighed and hugged his arm tighter. "Sorry, Jake, it's the SUVI. I felt them near yesterday, then they left when the storm hit. They didn't come back today. I guess I'm getting a bit twitchy and scared."

"Scared?"

"Yeah. As much as I'd love to be marooned here with you for a dozen years or so, I'm also terrified they'll give up on us and leave. Please just hold me for a minute until I get a grip on this."

To her great surprise he folded her into his arms and lightly kissed her hair. "It's okay, honey, I gotcha."

She snuggled tightly to him and allowed herself to enjoy this small closeness with him. She drew a few deep breaths to get control of her emotions then started to step away. Suddenly she felt the tremble in him. "Jake?"

"Sorry honey, I'm running out of fuel. Any chance you might cook up a lizard or two for a wounded warrior?"

With a laugh of delight, she stepped out of his arms, yet took his hand. "Right this way, big fella. We'll go see what the kitchen has to offer."

Jake was struggling when they reached the kitchen. It didn't look promising; something had broken in and cleaned up most of the meat.

Sinking into an oversized chair, he sat gasping for breath while Twenty set about seeing what she could salvage.

By the time she'd scraped and cleaned a few scraps of meat and some veggies, put them in a pot of water to boil, Jake was asleep, his head pillowed on his forearms. She smiled and lightly ran her fingers through his hair, then returned to her makeshift stew. "Dammit, this is not going to be easy."

A sigh escaped her lips as her reverie went on. "No it isn't, but I have to do this for the greater good. However, right now, he's mine, he's hurt, and I need to look after him, get him healthy again. And damn it, I'm allowed to enjoy it.

"If they don't come for us I could keep him. No, that would be worse, I'm already fighting the desire to run out looking for more SUVI. If they abandon us here poor Jake will be saddled with a super powered nut case. No fun at all for either of us.

"Nope, Tara my girl, this is going to be like when we lost Mom and Dad, only worse because he'll still be walking around where we can see him. Should we just go cold on him now, see if we can push it back?"

At that point he groaned and shifted his weight on the chair. Her heart leaped, and she fought the urge to leap to his side. "No, screw it. For the next few hours, or days, he's all mine. I'll squeeze every ounce of joy out of this as I can, then I'll bite the bullet and let him go when I have to, for the greater good.

"The Reacher needs stability from the leaders and getting between Jake and Carla would badly disrupt that. Like it or not, once we're rescued, I have to step aside. Sometimes life just sucks."

He groaned and sat up to see her turn and flash him a bright smile. "Hang in there, big fella, while I find us some tools and utensils to eat this with."

Chapter #9

Waiting Out the Storm

Once again Friendship hung in a low orbit above the location where Jake and SUVI 20 had disappeared. The SUVI hunters sat waiting, for there was little enough they could do until the storm abated. Carla Marks had come along as medic, and she was pacing impatiently.

"Carla, please come sit with us, you're making me dizzy."

"Sorry, Jeannie."

"What's eating at you, my friend?"

"Oh, nothing really, just worried about Jake."

"Do you not believe we will find them alive?"

"No, actually, I expect we'll find them alive ... together ..." She sighed and slumped into one of the small seats.

"Is that a bad thing?"

"I don't really know. I know she's been all over him for weeks, and I know he's a man. I can't imagine any man being able to resist those super SUVI pheromones."

"I don't understand. What are pheromones?"

Amanda took pity on Carla at that point. "Pheromones are how a woman signals a man she's ready to mate, Jeannie." Suvi-jean gave her a quizzical look, so she went on. "You know, honey, a girl likes a guy, she flirts with him, makes eye contact, moves into his personal space, that sort of thing.

"When that happens, her body sends out a scent, very subtle, but there, and even though he isn't aware of it, a man will respond, or his body will."

"Seriously? And you think the SUVI have an enhanced ability to do this?"

Carla rolled her eyes at that. "Oh, come on, Jeannie. Surely you must have noticed that, especially when you were a teenager. I'll bet there wasn't a man around who could resist you if you wanted him."

"You mean for sex?"

"Yes."

"Carla, believe me when I say I have no idea what you're talking about. No SUVI girl would ever attempt to get the attention of a human male. We feared and loathed them, and under no conditions would we try to draw their attention."

"Oh gods, Jeannie, I'm sorry, I completely forgot. I'm so sorry."

"You believe we have this ability?"

"Every woman does."

"And you think our, what did you call them, pheromones? You think our pheromones are stronger than normal humans?"

"Everything about you SUVI is stronger, Jeannie. Why would this be any different? SUVI 20 is like a teenager with her first real crush. She doesn't have your experiences of humans, so ..."

"You fear Jake will choose her over you as a lover."

"Yeah, that. Look at her, she gorgeous, and SUVI. He was all about you when you first came aboard the Reacher."

Amanda leaned closer to take Carla by the hand. "Honey, think for a minute. This is Jake we're talking about here. When was the last time anyone distracted him from a path he's chosen? Jake made you a promise, and pheromones or not, I don't see anyone turning him away from that or making him break that promise."

"Even if she a super sexy SUVI?"

"Even then, I just can't see it happening."

"Yeah, maybe, ... I guess. I'm fussing for nothing?"

Jeannie also patted her hand. "Thirteen would say don't borrow trouble, enough will find you without help. Relax and be ready when we find them. We do know he's injured, and he'll need her to protect him, keep him alive."

"Yeah, I guess." She sighed and leaned back in the chair. Amanda put an arm around her shoulders and hugged her.

Jeannie rose and went to where Dorind was working at his screen. "Got a minute for me?"

"Of course, Admiral. Congratulations on the promotion."

"Thank you. Now, of all the Earalith, you are the most widely travelled and experienced. Have you ever seen a planet like this before?"

"Yes and no. This has the look of an old mining world, probably operated by slaves mostly, then abandoned when the ore ran low. I've seen a few stormy worlds before, but nothing like this. Admiral, I believe most of the operation would have been underground. If our people have disappeared, perhaps that's where they went."

"I see. What should we expect to find if we locate an entrance to such a place?"

"Tunnels into the ground for mining purposes, storehouses, food and lodgings for the overseers as well as a few guards and supervisors. The slaves would probably be housed above ground."

"Oh, why?"

"Cheaper to put up the buildings. They found access to one of those didn't they? All they'd have found would be a big room with drinking water access. The food and other facilities would be underground, guarded.

"Admiral, you might also discover a hidden entryway to a landing site for supply ships and metal transporters. They'd want them underground to avoid being caught in one of those storms while loading valuable cargo."

"That's good information, Dorind, thank you. Tell me, can this ship's sensors detect those underground facilities?"

"Oh, yes, quite possibly. I should have thought of that. Shall I begin recalibrating the sensors?"

"Let me speak with your captain first, it will be her decision to make."

"It's a great idea and I like it. Go for it, Dorind. Sorry, Admiral, I couldn't help overhearing your conversation."

"No problem at all, Linsey, and thank you."

Jeannie turned back to see Carla with her head on Amanda's shoulder. Suvi-jean's heart went out to her as she could clearly remember how it had felt when she thought she'd lost Amanda. She sat down and put her arms around both of them.

SUVI 20 HAD SCROUNGED up some utensils and they took their time over the stew she'd created. Jake had to admit, it wasn't bad. Once they'd filled their bellies, she took his hand and led him back to the infirmary. "You're exhausted, big guy, you need to rest."

"So do you, sweet lady. You've been carrying the load for days now. Even a super SUVI can't run on empty forever, you need rest too. Just give me a minute here." He settled her in the chair then dragged a few heavy objects over and piled them across the doorway.

"Jake?"

"I know. This won't stop anything that really wants to get in, but it will slow them down and cause a racket. The noise will wake us up and you can beat them up for me."

She laughed at that then got a naughty twinkle in her eye. "Jake, are you suggesting we sleep together?"

"Absolutely." He grunted with the effort as he levered himself onto the wide oversized bed. "Come on, Miss Naughty, crawl up on this bed with me."

"Oh darling, now we're getting somewhere." She moved onto the bed like a stalking tigress.

Jake chuckled and folded her into his arms, snuggled her onto his good shoulder, and kissed her hair. "Behave."

"Jake?"

"You've got the twitchies; my SUVI girl needs a hug and a snuggle."

"Yeah, you're right there. It's been a while since I felt them near. They'll be back, Jake. They will."

"I know, sweetie, I know; Jeannie won't leave us behind. Cuddle down and get some rest."

She reached up to kiss his cheek. "Thanks, Jake. I did need this."

"Hush now, sleep."

"Yes, dear."

"Hush, dammit."

She giggled at that, then snuggled closer. In spite of herself, she was asleep before he was. Jake was right; she'd been pushing the edge of her endurance for too long.

Twice in the night he awoke to her whimpers. He cuddled her close, whispered soothing sounds, and she settled down each time. It was many hours later he awakened, all his instincts screaming of danger.

Twenty must have felt him stiffen, as she was instantly awake as well. Jake put his lips to her ear and whispered softly. "Easy now, we've got company. How's your night vision?"

"Pretty good. Let me squirm around a bit and see if I can get a look at our visitor." With a soft sleepy sound, she stirred slightly, but now had her head on his chest, her eyes half opened. "Oh crap. Slow and easy, Jake, let's sit up now, show them we mean no harm."

Jake sat up and saw two figures in the doorway, just outside the barrier he'd made. For a long moment the stared at each other, then they slowly began to lift their spears. In response, Jake slowly reached for the hand blaster. At sight of that, they suddenly fled.

"Well, that was exciting. Any idea what those things were?"

"I think we got it wrong, Jake. I don't think the slaves devolved at all. I think they were abandoned here and managed to survive. That skeleton I saw could be from folk like that. I think we just saw a couple of that skeleton's descendants."

"I'll bet you're right about that, and that's the good news."

"What's the bad news?"

"We're not alone down here, Twenty. Those guys were carrying spears. We need to be a lot more careful than we have been."

"Second that, big fella," she said as she gracefully slid off the bed and strode to the barricade, easily tossing it aside. "All right, today's main mission is weapons."

"Works for me." He slipped off the bed and reached for his walking stick/staff.

They ate the few remaining morsels of the last night's stew, then set out once again. Having crossed the metal storage area and finding nothing useful, they arrived at another corridor of doors. Jake started opening them. Little useful was found until they discovered the locked room.

"Dang, that looks like some kind of lock, I can't get it open."

"Let me try."

"Go for it, girl, I'll keep watch."

"Are they still there?"

"Still there. They've been shadowing us all day, but as soon as I look at them, they hide. Still, better they're shy than aggressive."

"Can't argue that," she replied as she inspected the lock. "Might as well try the easy way first." Twenty had found a long-handled hammer in the metal area and had kept it for a weapon.

Jake's eyes opened wide as she swung it over head then brought it down hard on the lock. The lock didn't break, but the door did. With the lock dangling from a series of wires, the door slid halfway open. With a grin of delight, Twenty squeezed into the opening then pushed the door the rest of the way open. "Wow, I guess my daddy was right."

Jake gave her the raised eyebrow. "Excuse me?"

"He always said if what you were doing didn't work, get a bigger hammer."

Jake's great bellow of laughter sent their observers scurrying for cover and brought a bright smile to her face. "Your father was a wise man indeed, Twenty. So, what do we have behind the magic door?"

"You're not going to believe this."

"Oh?"

"Looks like a locker room. Probably for the mine guards."

"Oh? Why the guards and not the miners?"

"Locked door?"

"Yeah, I guess. Okay, let's explore a bit." They began to poke around, looking into a few lockers and such. They found no weapons, but Jake found a bonanza, the shower room. It had been days and days since they'd been able to clean up. With fingers crossed, he gave it a try. <Water.>

There were a few creaks, groans, and sputters from the ancient system, then it began to dribble from the shower heads. The trickle slowly became a stream of brackish water then it began to clear. Jake stuck his hand in and grinned. <Increase temperature three degrees.> He gave it another minute then tried again. "Oh yeah, that's what I've been missing."

He grinned even wider as he called out. "Twenty, come here."

The reply came from further into the locker room. "What did you find?"

"Come and see. Girl, you're going to love this."

She came hurrying around a bank of lockers. "What is it, Jake, did you find ... is that a shower running?"

"Surprise."

"Oh dear gods, hot water."

"You go first, honey. I'll keep an eye on the door, so our friends don't peek."

"Oh to hell with it, Jake; come in with me. I don't care if they watch."

He blushed to his roots at her naughty grin. "Woman, you're bad. Behave yourself and get into that shower."

"Oh come on, get in with me, you know you want to."

"Behave, dammit." Her sweet laughter made him blush even deeper. She started stripping off her clothes. "I'll be watching the door."

"You could watch me too, if you want."

"Twenty, for the love of mercy, will you stop; you're killing me here. Behave." Her laughter made him smile as he turned away to watch the entrance. *"She'll never know how badly I want to get in there with her. Dang woman doesn't make it easy."*

SUVI 20 stepped under the cascading water and groaned with delight. "Oh god, hot water feels so damn good. Now to get the crud from the other day washed out of my hair."

It was a long time later he felt a soft touch on his shoulder. He turned to see a freshly scrubbed SUVI 20, wet hair falling down her back, smiling brightly up at him. Unconsciously, he almost reached for her, but she put a hand on his chest. "Oh no, you don't. You get your butt in that shower, mister."

"Right, shower." He passed her the hand blaster then stepped past and went to the shower. The shower system had been designed for Earalith, so it was too short for Jake's six-foot three-inch frame. He had to squat down a bit to wash his hair, but it was worth it. After scrubbing himself clean as he could, he took a few minutes to just enjoy the water, then reluctantly stepped out.

"The blower is just to your left."

"Blower?"

"A warm air blower, dries you off, no towels."

"Oh." Suddenly he realized she was right behind him. He turned to see her grinning at him as she handed him his clothes. She licked her lips then turned and fled. Muttering to himself he dressed then sought her out. He found her watching the door. "Brat," he growled as he kissed the top of her head.

"Are you going to spank me for being naughty?"

"I would but you'd probably like it."

Her laughter brought a chuckle from him, but she swiftly turned away toward the door. "Company's coming. I'll hold the door; you find us another way out of here."

"Yes, ma'am." He moved quickly as he searched for another exit. "Locker room, I wonder, did they have weapons here? Did they leave any for us to find?" They had, he found it on the second door he tried.

Jake looked over what he'd found. They looked something like a gun but built for smaller hands and grooved for two thumbs. He tested one, but the charge must have been depleted. The batons and clubs were familiar, and he grabbed two then hurried back to the door to find Twenty facing off with a half dozen lizard folk with spears. Just as he arrived, they dropped a dead animal then thrust a young female towards them. They pointed at Twenty then waited.

Twenty's heart soared as Jake stepped in front of her. "You can forget that, she's mine and I'm keeping her."

They didn't understand what he'd said, but him gently guiding her behind him spoke volumes. One of them stepped closer, motioned to the kill and to the female, then at SUVI 20. Jake shook his head. "You get to Twenty over my cold dead body." The creature raised its spear; Jake raised the hand blaster. "I said no, man. No means no."

He gently patted the young female on the shoulder then tried to steer her back to her own people. The lizard men raised their spears to prevent her return. She whimpered slightly then Twenty reached past Jake and pulled the girl behind him with her for protection.

Jake took a step forward. "You guys are acting like assholes, so here's the deal. Take your kill and bugger off, no hard feelings. You don't want the girl, fine, we'll keep her. You want Twenty? I'll never let that happen, so now it's your move."

They didn't understand the words, but got the message. The big one suddenly lunged at him with the spear. Jake batted it aside and cracked him across the head with the hand blaster. The creature staggered back. They all stood still looking at Jake. He pointed down the tunnel. "Go." They left.

As soon as they were out of sight, he turned to his companions. The female was cowering beside Twenty who was smiling sweetly at him. "What?"

She reached out to pat his arm, but the expected tease didn't come. "Thanks, Jake. So, what's our next move? What do you want to do with the girl?"

"The girl? You mean this one? I don't know, any ideas?"

"We could try asking her."

"Sure, why not?" He turned his attention to the female. "I suppose it would be too much of a stretch for you to know our language. How about Earalith?" <What is your name?> She turned her head from side to side, gazing at him with those large unblinking eyes. "Okay, so no Earalith either. Let's try something else."

Holding her attention, he reached out to pat Twenty on the shoulder. "Twenty." She didn't respond so he tried it again, nodding at her.

After a long moment she opened her mouth and a soft hissing voice sounded. "Tentee."

"Twenty."

"Tentee."

Jake patted his own chest. "Jake. Twenty, Jake."

The saurian girl nodded eagerly. "Tentee, Kake."

SUVI 20 snickered at that. "Shut up, Twenty. Twenty, Jake, ...?" He was holding his hand out toward her.

She got the idea. Eagerly she pointed to Twenty, "Tentee, Kake, Sessas." She brightened as she patted her own chest. "Teentee, Kake, Sessas."

Twenty was smiling now. "Okay, step one taken, now what?"

"I'm beat and my shoulder hurts. I should have shot that bugger instead of braining him. What do you think, make camp here or try to get back to the kitchen?"

"Kitchen's a long hike away, Jake honey, and there's no food left there. Let's keep exploring and see if we can find something closer."

"Works for me." Jake started toward another door to investigate.

As he stepped away, Sessas gave a squeak, whipped out a small knife and began skinning out the dead animal. She was hissing and grunting at them the whole time. They had no idea what she was saying, but it was clear she didn't want to leave the meat behind.

She swiftly skinned it out and cleaned the carcass, then threw it over her shoulder. Rising to her feet she gestured at Jake with her fingers, indicating he should lead on. The grin of mischief on Twenty's face caused him to roll his eyes as he started out. Three doors later he found it, another small kitchen, one probably reserved for the guards.

Twenty poked around, found what she needed, they soon had the meat cooking, while Jake tried to get comfortable in one of the small chairs. Eventually he gave up and sank to the floor. Twenty noticed and came to check on him. "The hip wound?"

"Yeah, I've been on my feet too long today. Thanks for not wanting to go back to the old kitchen."

"It's okay. Here, lay your head back on my jacket while I finish cooking the meat."

"Twenty, are you all right?"

"Sure, why do you ask?"

"You're not tormenting me. I thought you might be coming down with something."

"You're tired, honey, I'll tease you again tomorrow." She kissed the top of his head, then returned to what she'd been doing.

Sessas had been watching her closely. She scooted over to Jake, touched the top of his head with her muzzle, then picked up one of the clubs he'd found and stepped to the door where she settled down to watch for intruders. Jake saw the impish grin on Twenty's face and sighed. "Shut up, Twenty."

He smiled and closed his eyes at her delighted laugh. He lay dozing until she announced the meat was ready. They sat and each ate a small portion. Sessas bolted hers then returned to her watch post. Jake and Twenty were speculating on a rescue by the SUVI when Sessas hissed a warning.

A quick glance over her shoulder and Jake saw the approaching lizard men carrying spears. Grumbling he drew the hand blaster and stepped out into the corridor to face them. Twenty appeared at his right, her long handled hammer in her hand. Sessas stepped to his left, a club at the ready. The spearmen began to run toward them.

"These guys are starting to get on my nerves," growled Jake. He waited until they were close enough then he pulled the trigger. All five of the enemy spearmen were flung head over heels backwards for several feet.

As they picked themselves up and tried to clear the cobwebs Jake shouted at them. "You assholes get the idea now?"

Sessas' voice sounded right beside him. "Assholesss."

"That word she gets right," sighed Jake as Twenty snickered.

The biggest of the spearmen got to his feet, retrieved his spear, then pointed at Twenty then down to his side, indicating she should go to him. Jake was having none of it. He stepped forward and raised the blaster. "Get it through your head, Twenty's my girl; I won't let you have her. Now bugger off." He fired again, and the creature was sent tumbling over and over down the tunnel.

Jake was still muttering as he turned around and saw the sweet smile on Twenty's face. "Dang fools never learn ... what?"

"'Twenty's my girl, I won't let you have her?'"

"Oops. Twenty ..."

"Hush now, Jake. I know what we have to do as soon as we're rescued. Just let me enjoy the title, just for the few hours we have left here. Okay?"

Gently he folded her into a hug and kissed the top of her head. "Yeah, it's okay honey, but it's going to make this harder."

"I know," she replied as she snuggled closer. "Don't care."

At that point Sessas squirmed between them, making a purring sound, and stretching her head up toward Jake. "I think she wants a hug and a kiss on the noggin, too," giggled Twenty.

"Oh for pity's sake." With a chuckle, Jake hugged the Saurian girl and kissed the top of her head. She gave a soft squeal of delight, hugged him harder, then darted away to her guard post at the door. Noticing the naughty grin he was getting from Twenty, he shook a finger at her and rolled his eyes.

Chapter 10

Rescued

Linsey da Silva yawned as she emerged from her cabin, SUVI 18 close behind her. She smiled as she settled into the captain's chair. "What's the good word people?"

"The storm below is abating at last, Captain," replied Ettelan as he checked the sensors then took his place at pilot.

"That's good news."

"There's more good news, Captain da Silva."

"Oh, talk to me, Dorind."

"I couldn't sleep so I arose and returned to the sensors. I have located and mapped much of the underground mining complex. Once I got started, Ship recalled having been here once before. He was able to locate the landing bay for me. We have much to share with Admiral Sorenson when she awakens."

"Somebody call for an admiral?" asked Jeannie, as she emerged from the cabin.

Dorind smiled with delight as he delivered his report. He called up the map of the mining complex for Jeannie to inspect. "So, this area here is where the landing bay is located?"

"Yes, Admiral, this is a saurian world, most are like this to one extent or another."

"Saurian world?"

"Mostly populated with lizards of one form or another. They would be augmented to work the mines."

"I see. Is this close to where we finished the other day?"

"No, when we were forced to leave the planet, the SUVI were here, a long way from the landing bay. Admiral, so much time has passed the landing bay may not be functional, or it could be buried under rubble. Also, if our people are down there, they would have entered by another passage. If they had opened the hangar bay, we would see that on our sensors."

"Understood, Dorind, and thank you. That's good work. Linsey, how is our storm doing?"

"Storm is abating, Admiral. It's still dark down there, but we should be able to land you in another hour or so."

"Good. Now, once we're on the ground, check out that landing bay, see if you can get it open. If not, contact Recovery and get them to have a look at it. There might be something worth salvaging down there. Moira's going to use up all our spare metal building Amanda a new ship. It would be good to find her another supply."

"Yes, ma'am, orders received and logged. Ettelan, take us down for a look."

"Going down, aye."

The small scout ship dropped down toward the planet's surface as the SUVI hunters readied their gear. "The winds are still strong, but dying off quickly," said Eighteen, who had taken over at sensors. "Sun's nearly up."

"Put us back where we left off," said Jeannie.

Linsey nodded to Ettelan who expertly guided the ship around a hill then landed it lightly on the sandy ground. "Ship has landed, Captain."

"We're here, Admiral. Once you're clear we'll check out the landing bay. Good hunting." The SUVI hunters dropped out of the hatchway then the ship rose into the air and sped away.

"There's no tracks left to follow, thanks to that blasted storm," said Jeannie. "We know there's an underground mining complex here; we know our own people have seemingly vanished. Eighteen suspects they are in the complex, as she's certain they're both alive.

"So, don't worry about looking for tracks, spread out a bit and look for a way into that complex. It shouldn't be far as we know they were here, and one was injured."

With a quick nod the SUVI spread out and began to search. It wasn't long before SUVI 12 gave the call, she'd found the hole where Jake had fallen through. As the others raced to her so did something else. The huge predator that had chased Twenty down the hole.

Twelve dropped through the hole as the others converged on the predator, weapons blazing. With a roar of pain and protest, the monster fled. "Twelve?"

"Down here, Five. They were here all right, there's a comm unit on the floor. I think they were trying to charge it up."

"Coming down." A moment later the remaining four SUVI hunters were in the tunnel with Twelve. A quick look around showed Jeannie the long tunnel and broken comm. "Two, Twelve, and Thirteen, go that way. Nineteen and I will go this way. Stay in touch on comms." Without another word the hunters separated and began their search.

TWENTY SAT UP WITH a gasp. She'd been cuddled in Jake's arms while Sessas watched the door. "Twenty, what is it?"

"They're here, Jake."

He sighed and reached for the hand blaster. "Dammit anyway."

"No, Jake honey, the SUVI, they're here, in the tunnels. They're back where we fell in, searching, but it won't take them long to find us."

"Damn, I wish we still had a functional comm unit. We need to warn them about the assholes with spears."

She chuckled and hugged him tightly. "These are SUVI hunters, Jake. If those morons with spears go at them they're in for a rude surprise."

"Yeah, I guess you're right. I've seen what Jeannie and Thirteen are capable of. Okay, so I guess we should be expecting company soon."

Suddenly he saw the look on her face and almost reached for her. She put her hand on his chest to stop him. "For the greater good, Jake. We have to do this; I just wish I'd had a bit longer to enjoy my title."

"Twenty ..."

"No. There's no winning this one, and you know it. You still love Carla, and now me, I can feel it. The problem here is you and Carla are both important people, important to the wellbeing and success of the Reacher, the survival of us all."

She stopped speaking and drew a long ragged breath. "Just promise me I'll get a sisterly hug and a kiss on the noggin once in a while."

Jake pulled her close and kissed the top of her head. "I wish to all the gods of man I could see a way through this where nobody gets hurt, but I can't."

"It's okay, Jake. I'm SUVI tough, I can take it. Besides, I started this mess in the first place. It's all my fault and I'm sorry for it. Come on now, give me another kiss on the noggin then let me go."

He hugged her tightly and kissed her hair, but before he could release her Sessas wriggled between them and stretched up her head for a kiss. Laughing, both Jake and Twenty hugged her and kissed the top of her head.

"WHAT DO YOU THINK, Five?"

"They were here all right, and they stayed for a while. We saw where they cooked food, and now this. This must be where Twenty patched up Jake's wounds. The question now is, where would they go?"

"Exploring, searching for another food source or weapons. We found the big blaster where they came in. Without that they must have run low on weapons. Neither is a SUVI hunter; so they'd be looking for more effective weapons."

"Makes sense to me." Jeanie reached for her comm unit. "Five to Thirteen."

"Here, Five."

"We found where they were, but still no sign of them. You?"

"Nothing. This way leads down into the mine. We've reached the point where building ends and dirt mine begins. There are a lot of tracks, but none belonging to a human or SUVI."

"Understood. Come back to us and we'll renew the search from here."

"Do you think they might return here?"

"I don't know, Nineteen. They were here for a while, so they might."

"If they don't get here before the hunters, I'll leave my comm unit where they'll see it. That way, if we miss each other they can contact us."

Jeannie patted his shoulder as she stepped back to the corridor outside the infirmary. "That's good thinking, my friend. I like it." A few moments later the rest of the hunters arrived. "I see you've brought friends, Thirteen."

"Are they still there? I'm impressed they managed to keep up. Yes, Dorind called them saurians. We tried to talk to them, but if we look at them they disappear into side tunnels. We didn't try to follow as it's doubtful our people would have left the lighted areas."

"Agreed," sighed Jeannie. "All right let's assume they went this way. Check every door you find; they respond to the Earalith command to open."

They set out from there; Nineteen checked the first door and the others passed it by, each one checking another door. They soon found the entrance to the metal storage area. "They went through here," observed Jeannie. "There are tracks in the dust here for us to follow."

"There's enough metal here to build another two or three ships," mused SUVI 12.

Jeannie smiled at that. "You've been hanging around Engineering again. Yes, you're right, and I think that's a fine idea. First we find our people, then we bring Moira down here for a look."

"They wandered around down here a bunch, Five," said SUVI 2, "but here's where they left. There's another corridor out here."

SUVI 20 WAS FAIRLY dancing with excitement, and yet she was tormented as well. The SUVI were almost there, but now she would have to face the inevitable heartbreak. The voice of Sessas broke into her reverie. "Assholesss."

Both Jake and Twenty were at her side instantly. "Where?"

The Saurian girl pointed. "Assholesss, Kake." She said something else, but they couldn't understand it. They didn't need to; they could see the dozen or more spearmen advancing down the corridor.

Jake just shook his head and sighed. "Ah shit."

"Ssshit, Kake, assholesss."

"You can say that again," he grumbled, as he spun the short baton in his hand and reached for the blaster with the other. "Shut up, Twenty." That only changed her snicker to a full bodied laugh that brought a sloppy grin to his face.

The spearmen were advancing cautiously. Their last defeat had taught them to be wary of this strange creature, but their leader still wanted the female. Suddenly a door opened, and five SUVI charged through.

A glance showed Jeannie the situation and, as though controlled by a single mind, the SUVI changed course. Jake's voice stopped the impending massacre. "Whoa, stop. You don't have to hurt them, just show them your blasters, they'll run."

As one the SUVI fanned out to command the entire corridor, brandishing their weapons. The spearmen turned and vanished into a side tunnel. Jake stepped out and caught Jeannie in his arms. "Took your time getting here, Little Sister."

"Jake, I'm so sorry it took so long to find you. Those damned storms ..." She got no further as Sessas wriggled between them, lifting her head up to Jeannie. "What ...?"

"She wants you to kiss her on the top of the head."

Jeannie smiled at the eager young creature gazing up at her. She gave her a kiss on the head and, with a soft squeal of delight, Sessas slipped away to stand guard at the door. Jeannie shook her head bemusedly, then SUVI 20 wriggled between them. "I want a hug too."

With a laugh Jeannie hugged her too then kissed the top of her head. Jake stepped back and indicated the rest of the SUVI should join the group hug. As they moved close to her, Twenty burst into tears.

"You were alone too long, my sister," said Jeannie, as she tightened her arms around the shaking girl. "The storms held us at bay, or we'd have been here much sooner."

"Doesn't matter," sniffed Twenty. "You came back for us, that's what matters. Jake held me together, especially each time you left the planet. The big guy figured it out, you should probably keep him."

Jeannie laughed at that. "Yes, our big brother is pretty smart at that, we'll keep him."

"My lucky day," grinned Jake, but the guard on the door sounded the alarm again.

"Assholesss."

"They're back? What do they want?" asked Jeannie.

"They want Twenty, but they're bloody well not getting her," growled Jake, as he took the big blaster from SUVI 12 and stepped out the door. "Last chance, Assholes. Beat feet or fly." The spearmen were still out of reach of a hand blaster, but the big scatter blaster reached them with ease, sending them flying and tumbling back down the corridor.

He stepped back inside where SUVI 12 grinned at him as he passed back the weapon. "What?"

"Nothing, nothing at all." She was still grinning, Twenty was blushing, and Jeannie was looking at him with a strange expression. He didn't say anything else, just handed back the blaster.

Sessas snuggled under his arm. "Assholesss."

"You got that right," he sighed as he gave her shoulders an affectionate squeeze then kissed the top of her head.

Jeannie grinned at them. "I think I need to get you back to the Reacher for a checkup, and I want to introduce your new girlfriend to Linsey and Eighteen. Twenty, have you guys explored much down here?"

"We did a bit, but the real bonus was the metal storage area. We also found and activated the showers; that was great. If you want, I'll stay down here with the salvage crews. I assume you'll want to explore the place further."

"I'd like that, but first I want you to get checked out on the Reacher." She grabbed her comm unit. "Sorenson to Friendship."

"Friendship here, Admiral."

"How's it coming with that access bay?"

"The crew of Recovery One is digging it out now. Shouldn't be a lot longer."

"Sounds good, Linsey. We've found our people, and I want to send them back to the Reacher for a quick checkup. I also have someone here you'll want to meet. Can your magic engineer locate us?"

"Dorind here, Admiral. Return to the corridor and turn right. The second door on the right will lead you to the docking bay. We should be able to meet you there momentarily."

"Excellent work, people. On our way."

SUVI 12 led the way with Sessas beside her. She was trying to teach the girl the word *hostiles*, but without a spearman to use for demonstration purposes, it seemed like a lost cause. She got the word easily enough but had no context for it.

They entered the bay just as the huge doors began to open. Sessas squealed in fright and hid in Jake's arms. He put his arm around her and made soothing sounds. "Hush now, Sessas, hush. It's okay, these folk are friends."

"Fenesss."

"That's right, friends. Here they come now. You'll love Linsey, she'll want to talk to you a lot."

"Fenesss, Linsssey."

"That's right, Linsey."

At that point Friendship swept into the hangar and alit beside them. The hatch flew open, and Carla hopped down to leap into Jake's arms, locking her lips on his. Jeannie noticed the sad look on Twenty's face as she looked away, and her heart broke for the girl. She remembered what that felt like.

Carla was hugging Jake tightly, saying his name over and over while he held her tightly and kissed the top of her head. Predictably, Sessas squirmed between them and raised her head for a kiss on the head too.

"What the hell???"

"Easy, Carla, easy, she wants to be friends. She wants a hug and a kiss on the noggin. Sessas, this is Carla."

"Carsssa."

"That's as close as she'll get. Give her a quick squeeze and a smack on the noggin."

"Oh for pity's sake." Carla hugged the Saurian girl and kissed the top of her head. Sessas squeaked with delight and scampered away to Twenty.

"Who or what the hell is that, Jake?"

"Apparently, my new girlfriend. There's a group of them down here and they tried to trade her for Twenty."

"So you kept them both, right? It seems you weren't that hurt after all, just staying down here to chase the girls."

"Well sorta, there was this animal that tried to eat me, then I fell down a hole and blacked out for a while, and then those assholes showed up with Sessas, and ..."

"Oh just get in the ship," chuckled Carla. "I want to get you back to the Reacher and check you out."

Jake started toward the ship then turned to Jeannie. "Did I hear that right, you're an admiral now?"

"Long story, Jake," she grinned. "You need to stick around more."

"Gods, I go camping for a couple of days and look what happens. Jeannie, all jokes aside, you know of the metal storage because you came through there, and you know about the guys with spears. There could be more surprises down here. Before you let Recovery go crazy down here, let me get patched up then I can come down with a troop of Security guys to protect them."

"I'll do it," said Twenty as she joined them.

"Twenty?"

"Look, Jake, you need time to heal, and you need time with your lady. Your brother can lead the men down here and I can come with them, show them what to watch for."

"Walk with me, Twenty," said Jeannie, as she took the girl by the hand and led her aside for a moment. Jeannie put her arms around her and hugged her. "I can feel your pain, my sister, and I believe I know the cause of it. I have felt that pain before."

Twenty gazed into her eyes for a moment then sighed and laid her head on Jeannie's shoulder. "It's my own damn fault, Captain, I mean, Admiral. He needs time to heal, time with her to heal that rift, and I think I need some distance to see if I can heal."

"I understand. I'll speak to Sheila, and you will accompany whoever returns as escort for the salvage teams. Twenty, my sister, if you ever have need ..." She got no further as Sessas wriggled between them. Both Jeannie and Twenty laughed, hugged her and kissed the top of her head.

"SUVI 5 since the first moment we met you have been so good to me, and I love you for it. You're friends with Jake and Carla too, I won't put you in the middle of this mess, but thank you. I may need a shoulder to cry on once in a while, but I'll talk to Antha."

"Twenty, you are precious to me, to all the SUVI. We are all here for you."

"Thank you. Now, I think I should introduce Sessas to Linsey, what do you think?"

"Capitol idea, let's go."

They were the last to board the ship and Linsey was waiting for them. "Jake, introduce me to your girlfriend."

"Of course, Captain da Silva. Sessas, this one is Linsey."

"Linssseee."

Linsey put her arms around the girl and kissed the top of her head. Sessas chirped with delight and enthusiastically returned the hug. "Did I get it right, Jake?"

"You did, Linsey. She likes you."

"And I like her. You say she has a rudimentary language?"

"Far as I can tell."

Jeannie smiled then spoke up. "Let's get back to the Reacher, then you can play, Linsey."

"Yes, ma'am. Eighteen, my love, take over the ship and get us home. I'm going to sit here with Sessas and see if I can get some of this language."

Chuckling, SUVI 18 settled into the captain's chair. "Ettelan, take us home, if you please."

"Homeward we go, Captain Eighteen," he grinned.

The small ship lifted off and moved outside into the winds, but soon rose above them then shot toward the Reacher.

Chapter 11

Hard Times

As soon as Friendship landed in the belly of the Reacher, Carla hustled Jake and Twenty off to the medical bay. Sessas hung back with Linsey. Carla gave Jake a full going over, muttering the whole time. "What were you thinking?"

Jake took her into his arms and kissed her softly. "Easy, sweet woman, easy. I'm all right, I survived and made it back. It's all right."

She burst into tears and buried her face against his shoulder. "Oh Jake, I was so afraid I'd lost you. It would just kill me to lose you."

"You didn't lose me, sweetheart, and you never will. I'm right here, it's all okay."

"I know. Okay, let me have a look at you. Wow, you took a real beating, Jake. This is healing well, so is this. Who stitched up this wound, Twenty or Sessas?"

"Very funny, Miss Super Medic. You know it was Twenty. That sweetie saved my life a dozen times over, Carla, and risked her own to do it."

"Yeah, I guess I'm just being a jealous bitch. She really did do a good job here for a woman with no formal medical training. I'll just give you a shot of the good stuff to make sure you didn't bring any new bugs onto the ship." She gave him the injection then kissed his cheek. "I'll go check out Twenty now. You get dressed and we'll go to the mess for some real food as soon as I'm finished."

He nodded and reached for his shirt. "Can we go by quarters, so I can get a shower and clean clothes first?"

"Absolutely."

She kissed him again then stepped out of the cubicle and over to the next one where SUVI 20 was waiting. As she stepped in Twenty was sitting on the bed, staring at her hands. "Are you going to shoot me?"

"I'll admit, the jealous part of me wants to, but the sensible part of me says no. I owe you far too much for that. I can easily tell by those healing injuries that he couldn't have survived on his own. You kept him alive and brought him back to me. Let me check you out now."

A few moments later she sighed and passed Twenty her shirt. "You're in remarkably good shape. Must be that SUVI healing factor. Jake didn't tell me you'd been injured too."

"He didn't know. He was unconscious most of that time, we were out of ammo and food. I had to kill something the hard way."

"I see."

"Carla, listen to me. That damned virus that made me SUVI also threw me back into puberty. I know I've been chasing after your man like a teenager with her first crush. You're jealous, and you have every right to be.

"However, you need to know this. I gave Jake every opportunity, and encouragement, yet he turned me down. He hugged me so I wouldn't go bat-shit crazy when the SUVI left the planet, called me little sister, kissed the top of my head, and told me to behave. At no point did he ever betray your trust."

Carla sighed and leaned back against the table. "Thanks for that. Is that where Sessas got the kiss on the head thing from?"

Twenty chuckled at that. "Yes, she squirmed in between us and wanted a snuggle too. Jake tried to teach her a few words, like our names and such, but it's hard for her. When the bad guys showed up Jake called them assholes. She got that one right."

Carla smiled. "Yeah, I heard her use that one. Okay, Twenty, you're good to go. All you need is a few good meals."

"And a shower and clean clothes?"

"Wouldn't hurt. Jake and I are headed for the mess, meet us there?"

"I'll pass. I think I need a shower and two days sleep more. Rain check?"

"Any time."

Carla left and Twenty sighed deeply. She'd heard Jake call her sweetie as he told Carla of their adventures. She'd been surprised at the strength of her reaction to it, and how deeply she ached to hear it again. This was not going to be easy. Apparently, SUVI loved harder than humans too. She pulled on her clothes and headed to her quarters.

Twenty opened her door to find Antha and three SUVI, Jeannie, Eighteen, and Four, waiting for her. "What's up? You guys start the party without me?"

Antha didn't speak, just stepped into her arms, and hugged her tightly. Twenty returned the hug as the SUVI joined in. No one spoke, they just held her. Twenty started to tremble, then the tears started. Great wracking sobs shook her body until she fairly melted into their embrace.

When the storm of emotion passed, Four led her to the couch and settled down with her. "You go on, Five, you have a ship to run. Eighteen and I will stay with her. Antha, Morthel will be looking for you."

"Yes, Momma Four," smiled Antha, as she and Jeannie left the room.

While Eighteen and Four stayed with Twenty, filling the need for SUVI closeness within her, easing the loneliness, Jeannie called a senior staff meeting. "All senior staff to the bridge. All captains to the bridge. Passenger representatives to the bridge." She arrived to find most of them already there.

As soon as they were all assembled, she called them to order.

"All right let's get started, we've regained all our people from the surface of the planet. Now let's find out where we stand. First Officer Hoffman?"

"Of course, Admiral. All's been fairly quiet aboard the Reacher. We found nothing of particular interest on the fifth and sixth planets of this system before we were recalled to assist Explorer. It's all good from here."

"Carla, how are our refugees doing?"

"Jake will need a few days of rest then he should be fit for duty, but it will be a few weeks before all his injuries are fully healed. SUVI Twenty is in remarkably good shape. A good night's sleep, a hearty meal, and she's good to go. Mr. Sacumbtu and his men are already back on the job."

"Good to know. People, we got off easy with this one, things could have been a lot worse. Linsey, how is our new mascot doing?"

Linsey chuckled at that. "Sessas is all curiosity, Admiral. She's managed to install the kiss on the head with most of my crew and a number of the Reacher's crew as well."

"Any progress with her language?"

"I'm starting to get a sense of it. Language is difficult for them, and they use a lot of subtle body language as part of their communications. She was a slave whose people tried to trade for SUVI 20. Jake refused and drove them away, but protected Sessas as well.

"She interpreted Jake hugging Twenty and kissing her on the top of the head as a sign of love. By her understanding of the way the world works, she offered herself as his second ... concubine seems to be the word closest to it. Anyway, by her standards, he accepted.

"After a while, when she didn't see them physically mating, she decided the noggin kiss was a sign of affection for family. Every time someone goes along with that, she accepts them as family ... perhaps clan might be the right word. Anyway, it's still a work in progress."

"Keep at it, Linsey, I'd like to know more about this, about her. When we found Jake and Twenty there were a number of her people with spears approaching. Jake had fought them off before. We also found a large amount of Earalithian metal down there, and I'd rather not have to fight off her people for every scrap of it."

"Did you say Earalithian metal?"

"Yes, Moira, I did. There's a large storage facility full of it. It's underground, but we believe we can get a ship in there to access it."

"Just how much metal are we talking about here?"

"Enough to build three Explorers or more, Moira."

"You're serious? Oh, the gods are good to me. We can build them with the new engines, some extra Earalithian tech, and ... you are serious about building them, aren't you?"

"Yes, if it can be done. Can it be done?"

"Aye, if we have enough metals. We can fabricate everything we need if we have enough metal. We'll need a labor force, how about the passengers? What do you think, Miriam? We'll provide on the job training."

Miriam Holbrooke, spokeswoman for the passengers, smiled. "I'll put the word out, Moira. You'll be swamped within the hour."

Jeannie smiled at her eager Chief Engineer. "Well then, as soon as we're ready perhaps Linsey could take you down for a look, Moira. Take Twenty and Sessas with you, Linsey, as well as a strong security force. Give it a couple of days to work on the language thing with Sessas and to let Twenty rest up before you go.

"Now, about the ore hauler, is it ready?"

"It is," replied Moira Duncan. "She'll need a crew."

"Captain Volkov, you're in charge of recovery and salvage. What do you suggest?"

"Jeannie, I have a unique pair of men on my little ship. They discovered they work well together when we got hit with that blast. I say promote my first officer, give him the ship, and send Chance

Morita with him. Frank will pick a few from Reacher's crew to fly her, and Chance can gather up some of the bored passengers to get the planet-side work done."

"Seriously? All right, this one's your baby. They can report to you. You coordinate with Sheila for security people, with Moira once she's had a look at the goodies, and we'll go from there.

"Now, are there any items of interest from the passengers? Miriam?"

The woman chuckled and straightened in her chair. "The passengers are somewhat bored, Admiral, at least a number of the younger ones. The idea of getting an assignment to a salvage ship will have great appeal, same for the ship building crews. I'm sure Chance will have hundreds of applicants for the positions."

Jeannie nodded and smiled. "Perhaps this could be a bridge between the sky riders and grounders. It's all looking good. Moira, is that second Earalithian scout ship ready for service?"

"He's ready Captain. I know you've been holding him back in case any of the Earalith wanted to go their own way, but it looks like they'll stay with us. Do you want to put him into service?"

"I'd like to give him to Amanda for an explorer until you get her new ship ready."

"All right. We'll have to get Linsey to introduce Amanda and crew so he'll accept the new Captain."

"Linsey?"

"Sorry, Admiral. When he was brought in, we linked him to Friendship, you know, to speed up the process. Now he believes I'm his captain too. I'll introduce Captain Drake as his new captain, no problem."

"You're giving me a temporary ship? Suvi-jean, what are you up to?"

"Sweet Amanda, I want you and Linsey to team up, search that planet for more mining operations. They wouldn't have shown up on your old scanners, but Dorind can calibrate the ones in Friendship 2 to find them. Don't try to land or explore them, just find them if they're there."

"Sounds like fun, when do we start?"

"How about now?"

"As you command, Admiral," grinned Amanda. "Come on, Linsey, introduce me to your buddy."

WHILE THINGS WERE LOOKING good from Jeannie's angle, they weren't quite so rosy from Jake's side. Carla had stayed with him for two days but had been called back to work; he was sitting by himself in quarters, brooding. The door chime pinged. "Yeah?"

"It's Hal."

"Come in."

The door slid open and Jake's brother walked in. "You look like shit."

"I feel like shit." Jake sighed and pulled the ring from his hand and tossed it to Hal.

With a grin of delight, Hal put the ring on. "Warned you."

"I know, but I had it under control, I did. How the hell was I to know she would follow me planet-side, and rescue me when an animal dragged me off for a meal?"

"Yeah, hard to see that coming, but maybe she did. So where did you lose control?"

"She found me, Hal. She found me, nursed me, saved my life a dozen times or more. I fell through a roof of some kind and passed out. It was a mining tunnel, dark as hell, I was injured and out of ammo with a big lizard gnawing on my leg. I woke up in her arms and knew deep inside I didn't want to be anywhere else."

"So, I was right?"

"You were right. There's not a man alive who could resist a SUVI woman if she wants him."

"Super SUVI pheromones?"

"Yeah, but that's not all of it. Oh, that'll get your attention all right, but there's more to it."

"More?"

"I think a SUVI loves harder than a normal human too, or something. Anyway, I told her we had to behave, and she agreed."

"For the greater good?"

"Yup, for the greater good."

"So, what about Carla?"

"That's the hardest part of all, Hal. I still love Carla too. The minute she jumped off that ship and into my arms, I felt complete again."

"So you're utterly in love with two women?"

"That about sums it up. Just shoot me now."

"Sorry, no time. I'm forming up a troop to go down with the Recovery's crew. What am I facing down there?"

"Lizard men with spears, as far as I know. They can run as fast as a SUVI, but they're no stronger than we are. They have an intimate understanding of what a blaster can do, but they don't give up easy."

"Okay, good to know."

"Hal ..."

"Yes, Twenty is going down with us. I promise you; those assholes will never get close to her. I'll be watching her back all the way."

"Thanks, brother."

"Look, Jake, I can see what she means to you, Carla too. I won't try to get in the middle here, but I will protect my new sister-in-law."

"Shut up, Hal." With a chuckle of delight, Hal slapped his brother on the shoulder then left to find his crew.

SUVI 20 SAT IN HER quarters, staring at the weapon's belt Jake's brother had made for her. It had a hand blaster, a side arm, one bladed weapon, and her long-handled hammer hanging on a clip. He'd called

it her war hammer. She smiled weakly at the memory. Her door pinged, and she called out for the visitor to enter. When she looked up, Jeannie was standing there.

"Hi, Admiral, what's up?"

"We're alone here, Jeannie is fine, my sister. Tara, I'm a bit concerned about you going back down to the surface."

"I'll be fine, Jeannie, but thanks for the concern. Can you tell me something?"

Jeannie smiled and sat beside her. "Sure. What would you like to know?"

"Since I first saw you, you've been like a big sister to me, and more. I remember how good it felt when you held me gently and tried to help me make sense of what was happening. I've always felt I was special to you for some reason."

"And so you are, very special to me, to all the SUVI, to all humanity."

"But how? Why? That's what I don't understand. What is it you think I can do? I know you expect something from me, and I'm terrified I'll fail and disappoint you. Please can't you tell me what I'm supposed to do?"

Jeannie smiled and gathered the girl into her arms. She came willingly. Jeannie kissed the top of her head and sighed. "You will not fail me, sweet sister, for you have already succeeded in good measure. Tara, the first thing I saw of you was the intense pain, yet the courage with which you faced it. I knew then you had the strength to defeat the virus and become SUVI.

"You're special to us all because, unlike us, you've never worn the slave collar, never faced the horrors of all that means. Tara, the rest of us all have, and as a result we both loathe and fear the humans. Yes, we're working our way past that, making friends, finding lovers within the Reacher's crew, but it's the grounders that are the problem.

"You don't have that fear, that loathing that makes your skin crawl at the sight of one of them, the rest of us do. You've already made friends among them. They don't sense that fear from you, and as a result they're losing their fear of you, of all SUVI, and that's making it a bit easier for the rest of us.

"Sweetie, you're the bridge between the SUVI and the humans. I hoped that you would be able to help pull us closer together, for we are kindred species, and we do need each other if we're to survive long term."

"Wow. Jeannie, I'm so sorry, but I think I've just screwed that up big time."

"By falling in love with Jake?"

"Falling in love with him, buggering up his marriage, making his human wife hate me, all SUVI ..."

Jeannie laughed and gave her another gentle hug. "Whoa there, easy girl. I love the big guy too, as a brother and a dear friend, and the same for Carla. You didn't break their marriage; you fell in love with a guy.

"That's not a crime. You saved the man's life, and that's won you big forgiveness from all of us, especially Carla. She's not your enemy, and she doesn't see you as an enemy.

"I can't help you with this thing as I have no real experience, but I do know how it felt when I thought I'd lost Amanda. I know your pain, and I'm here for you if you need a shoulder to cry on."

Twenty sighed and gave Jeannie a gentle squeeze. "What would Amanda say about that?"

"She sent me here, told me what to do for you. I was fussing, pacing around our quarters. She asked what was bothering me, so I told her. She told me to come here, hug you, hold you and talk to you if you wanted to talk, and to just hold you if you didn't."

"I don't think I truly understand."

"We, the SUVI, especially the younger ones, were infected as children then enslaved. We have no idea at all how to properly interact with humans on a personal level. We struggle to get past the fear and loathing thing, but then we still have no idea what to do. We ask our friends, learn from our lovers, and we especially watch you for more clues."

"Wow, and then I went and screwed it up."

Jeannie chuckled at that. "You didn't screw it up. Where is it written, in the big book of human behavior, that everything has to be perfect all the time?"

"So, what am I supposed to do, Jeannie? What exactly is it you want me to do?"

"I want you to live, live free and enjoy. Make mistakes, cry, laugh, win victories, and more. By this example the rest of the SUVI can see that it really is okay for them to enjoy life too, to choose their own path, mess it up, try again, and all that is okay to do."

"Wow, I'll say this for you, Admiral Suvi-jean Sorenson, you give one hell of a pep talk."

"Did it work?"

"Yes, big sister, it worked. I'm feeling a lot better now. Next time I hit a blue funk can I get another one?"

"Any time at all, little sister. Any time at all."

Chapter 12

Back Planet-side

The winds were picking up again as Friendship swept down and opened the hangar door. Lights flooded the hangar as Hal White leaped from the ship, followed by a troop of heavily armed security men and SUVI 20. Soon shouts of "Clear!" were heard, then the ship rose and left to make room for the much bigger ship.

Recovery One settled into the hangar, then the doors closed to keep the rising storm outside. Olga Volkov and Moira Duncan descended from the ship followed closely by Dorind, the Earalithian engineer. "What's our status, Ensign White?"

"Hangar bay is secure, Captain Volkov."

"Good work. All right, Twenty, lead on. Show us the treasure."

"Captain, if I may."

"Dorind?"

"There is another entrance to the storage area over here, one Miss Twenty might not have found before we arrived. It is through here the metals would have been hauled to the transporter. It should still be working."

Olga smiled at the earnest little man. "Show us, Dorind."

He turned in a different direction, but SUVI 20 flashed past him, swinging her war hammer. There was a crunching sound, blood splattered everywhere, and a large lizard lay dead at her feet. Hal was right beside her, scatter blaster in hand. "That all of them?"

"All I can see. Dorind?"

Dorind was playing the beam of a flashlight all around the area. "I see no more, SUVI 20. Thank you for saving my life." She smiled and patted his shoulder. "Give me another moment, Captain, and I'll have the lights on in this area of the hangar bay."

True to his word, the area was soon bathed in light. "This way over here is where the cargo ships would be placed. They land there where we did, get moved over here, that large door panel would be opened, and the metals brought out to be stored on the ship. <Storage Bay, Open>

With a groan of protest, it did, revealing the huge storage area, nearly full of metal sheets, to their eyes. <Lights>

The lights came up and Moira Duncan whistled with delight. "Oh yes, the gods are good to me. It'll take a few months, but we can give the admiral at least three more ships for her fleet. What do you think, Dorind?"

"Yes, Moira, I believe three will be possible. There might even be more metal deeper in the complex. I wonder why they abandoned it here?"

"I really don't care why they left us so much bounty, my friend. I'm just thrilled that they did."

Dorind soon found the machines he was looking for, moved Recovery over near the storage bay doors, then chose a carrier to move the metals. Of the five lift carriers there, only the one was still functional, but it was making life a lot easier for them.

"I'll say this for the Earalith," grinned Moira Duncan, "they built things to last."

Olga Volkov chuckled at that. "I have to agree. Just how much of their methods are you incorporating?"

"As many as we can. Dorind is teaching a night class for all engineers, attendance is mandatory. Everybody needs to know what and how we're doing this. It's taking our tech ahead by several generations. When I retire I plan to write a whole new set of manuals for modern engineering."

"Retire? You? That'll be a few generations from now."

Olga was grinning, and Moira chuckled. "Yes, well, I didn't say it would be any time soon."

As the security men stood guard over the workmen collecting the sheets of metal, Hal reached up to rub at an old wound on his shoulder. It still ached a bit whenever he got near dampness, and it was damp in the underground complex.

SUVI 20 had been standing beside him and noticed something that gave her a turn. "That ring, that's Jake's ring. Why do you have it?"

"Easy, my new sister, easy. I'll explain. This is our grandfather's ring. I wear it until Jake wins a bet, then he wears it until I win it back."

"Oh." She visible got control and looked away, embarrassed. "Sorry."

"It's okay, no harm done."

"You called me your new sister, why did you do that?"

"Because my big brother has deep feelings for you, you're precious to him, and thus to me too. I promised him I'd watch your back down here and keep those lizard guys away."

"Hal, Jake and I can never be together. I can't be your new sister."

"Sorry, you don't get a choice there. Jake loves you, so, new sister. You're stuck with me."

She smiled and gently squeezed his arm. "I accept the adoption, Hal, and thanks. Dare I ask what the bet was?"

"I saw you flirt with him. He laughed it off, but I could see you were serious. I bet him there is no way any man could resist a SUVI girl who wanted him. I bet him he'd fall for you and get in a whole heap of trouble."

"What made you so sure?"

"The SUVI are super at everything. I was betting the SUVI love harder than humans too."

"Sadly, brother, you might be right about that. So, what's your take on all this?"

"Nope, not getting in the middle here, Jake's my brother, Carla and I have been close for as long as I can remember, and you're my new sister. I love you all and will protect you all, but I'll run like hell if the fur starts to fly."

She chuckled at that. "I wouldn't ask you to get in the middle, my new brother."

"Thanks for that, sweetie. Here."

She turned to see him holding out the ring. He'd taken the gold chain from around his neck and hung the ring on it. "Hal?"

"You knew this as Jake's ring. Wear it around your neck and a piece of him will always be with you. Just keep it under your shirt or I'll get shot at sunrise."

"Hal? Hal I can't ..."

To her surprise he pulled her close and kissed the top of her head. "Keep it, Twenty. It's okay." At that point Sessas wriggled between them and stretched her head up for a kiss on the noggin. They both laughed as they obliged her then watched as she scurried away to join Captain Volkov and the Chief Engineer.

WHILE HAL WAS ON THE ground with the crew of Recovery, Jake sought out a far corner of Engineering, the area where the armor for the security people was made. There was an older fellow there, humming to himself while he worked. He looked up and smiled as Jake entered. "Good afternoon, Sub-Commander White, what brings you to the bowels of the beast?"

"Looking for a way to avoid that very thing."

"Excuse me? I'm sorry, I don't understand."

"I was on a groundside mission with the crew of Explorer and got carried off by an animal. Standard armor kept me alive, but I took a number of injuries. My point is, our armor is designed to protect from projectiles and heavy blows, plus it has stun shields.

"However, it wasn't a lot of use against the constant pressure of an animal's jaws, plus it actually caused a few injuries when I took a bad fall. I'm hoping you can help me design something better for use on an unknown planet."

The old fellow's eyes twinkled with merriment. "Sounds like fun. How are you planning to test it?"

"The hard way. So, what do you say, want to give it a try?"

"Love to. I should tell you; I've been coming here to this work station for the past seventeen years, and in all that time, you're the first to ask for improvements in that armor."

Jake saw the mischievous grin on the man's face and matched it. "So, for the past seventeen years you've been designing new armor in your spare time?"

That brought a chuckle of delight. "Oh, indeed I have. I've also experimented with a few new materials, even made up a few prototypes. Want to see some?"

"Absolutely. Show me the goodies. Oh, call me Jake, I'll be spending a lot of time here in the near future."

"I'll enjoy the company, Jake. Name's Harlan. Now let me see, where did I put that Earalithian ... Ah, here we go. The ship they're calling Friendship 2 had a full locker of Earalithian armor. Apparently, he was a scout ship at one time.

"Here it is. I've used some of their material, and some of our own, as I scaled this up for a larger man. It still might be a little small for you but try it on."

He passed Jake a tunic of strange metallic material. "It will turn a projectile, has full stun shields, and more." Jake struggled into the garment. It was tight, but he managed it. "It'll turn a heavy blow as well, but here's the interesting part for you. This thing repels pressure."

"Repels pressure?"

"Ah-huh. Let's say you tripped and a boulder rolled onto you, the greater the pressure of the weight, the stiffer the material becomes to resist it. That animal of yours could chew on this all day and all he'd manage would be to break his teeth. It would also protect you from a long fall as it molds to the body, no soft spots or projections.

"Now, this shirt is a bit small for you. Give me a week and I can have a suit made up to fit you."

"Seriously? That would be awesome. Now what else have you got? Can you work this stuff into boots, gloves, and helmet?"

"Of course. Just who do you think you're talking to here?"

Jake roared with laughter. "Well, obviously, I'm talking to a genius of an armorer."

Harlan's eyes twinkled with merriment. "So, that's one suit of new armor. You want new weapons with that?"

"New weapons? Are you serious?"

"Absolutely."

"All right, magic man, show me what you've got."

"Actually, it's not new, just a few modifications on the standard stuff. This, for example. It's actually a much older design, but it will carry twice the number of rounds as a standard side arm. This smaller unit here is a more compact stunner, standard range. This one you'll love. It's a hand blaster with twice the range and three times the charge capacity. God bless Earalithian tech."

"Harlan, this is awesome. Look, I'll give this stuff a full field test, and if it's half as good as you say then I'll talk to Commander Singh about refitting the whole department."

"That would be great, I'd have enough to do to keep me entertained for weeks. So, want to something else amazingly useful?"

"There's more? Of course there's more. Show me the goodies."

"Got it right here. I call this the survival pack."

"Looks like a regular backpack."

"Works the same way, but it has a few more goodies in it. You see, on old Earth, there were folks who practiced the art of survival. This knife is one of their gadgets. It's a knife, saw, the end here is a compass in case the planet under investigation has a magnetic field.

"Now, unscrew the compass piece and inside you have a strong cord, plus a fire starter kit. See, flint and a steel. Just rub this along here to make sparks. This block of material is highly flammable. Let those sparks hit this and instant flames.

"Oh, one more thing about the armor, it will cool you off in the heat and will keep you warm and dry in the cold."

"Damn, Harlan, I sure wish I'd come talked to you before I went planetside. Twenty is going to love this fire starter."

"Oh?"

"She was down there with me, saved my life and kept me breathing. She used rocks, smashed them against the butt of a scatter blaster to get the sparks for a fire."

"Resourceful woman. Should I make up a full kit for her too?"

"Yeah, do that. She's about five foot eight, slim but athletic build."

"Got it. I can get the rest from ship's records. Give me a week then drop back."

"I'll be counting the days." Jake grinned as he left the area and returned to his quarters where he slowly fell back into his blue funk. He wondered how Twenty and Hal were doing.

THE LOADING OF METAL into the cargo hold of Recovery was going well. Security stayed close to the workmen, and Twenty, along with Hal and Sessas, patrolled the area's outer edges. It was good that they did. Sessas turned and grabbed Hal by the arm. "Asssholess, Hallll."

"Where?" She pointed into a darkened area by the wall. Flicking on his flashlight, he saw dozens of lizard men carrying spears appearing out of an unseen side tunnel. He grabbed for his comm even as the blaster leaped to his hand. "All security to my position, now."

The armed officers came running and formed a solid wall as the lizard men braced their spears. SUVI 20 appeared beside Hal, her war hammer in her hand. She recognized the lizard leader. "Assshole, Tentee."

Twenty nodded and patted Sessas on the shoulder. "Yes, that's him alright. He seems to be the leader of these fools."

"Yesss, Sossarr, lee derrr. Assshole."

"You can say that again," grumbled Twenty as the spearman stepped forward and pointed at her, then at the ground beside him.

Hal stepped forward, raising his blaster. "This woman is my sister; she is precious to me. Go away and no harm will come to you."

The creature hissed at him then glared at Twenty and pointed to the ground. She spun the hammer easily in her hand as she stepped up beside Hal. "You want me asshole, come try something. The war maiden is hungry."

She shook the weapon at him then leaped forward swinging the hammer. A large stone near the lizard man exploded under the power of that blow. "Keep pissing me off and that's your head."

Wide-eyed the creature watched as she stepped back beside Hal. For a long moment nothing happened, then it hissed something at Twenty and pointed to the ground beside it. Before anything else could happen, Sessas snatched a blaster from the belt of one security man, stepped forward and fired.

The leader of the spearmen went flying over backwards and the rest of them seemed to go into shock. Sessas waved the blaster at them then hissed something. They looked really nervous.

"Show them your blasters," commanded Hal. The entire squad raised their blasters, and the spearmen got the message. They faded back into the tunnel, leaving the leader behind. Reluctantly, he joined them.

"Assshole," muttered Sessas, as she returned the blaster to its rightful owner, hugged him, then stood beside Twenty and Hal.

Hal gazed at Sessas then grinned and hugged her. "I guess that solved that, Little Sister." He kissed the top of her head and she fairly wriggled with delight. "Twenty, war maiden? You named that hammer?"

"You started it. You called it a war hammer. I did a fast *history of weaponry* search and learned many warriors named their favorite weapons."

Hal just chuckled. "I like it. Now, tell me what you can about our little sister here. I notice she's always had a small crude knife on her belt. What's the story?"

"I have no idea. When she first joined us, she used the knife to skin out a dead animal for food. She seemed annoyed that Jake and I were just going to leave it there. I've never seen her show interest in any other weapon except a club. She sure has a dislike going for that big bugger though. I'm willing to bet she has good reason."

"Yeah, me too."

"Hal, what are you thinking?"

"I'm thinking our Sessas is a bit more mature than we realize. Her natural inquisitiveness and loving nature make us think of her as a child. I think that's wrong; I also think she and that big bugger have history."

"So?"

"So I'm going to give her a weapons belt, long blade, baton, and blaster only. I'm not sure she understands projectiles yet."

"You want to give her weapons? Why?"

"Twenty, my new sister, you saw what she did, and you know why."

"She was protecting me."

"Yes. I'd say that asshole has hurt her in the past, and she wasn't about to let that happen to you."

"Because I was the first to protect her. Jake tried to gently return her to her people, but she cringed away. I pulled her back with me, and he then defended us both. You're right, Hal, there's more to our Sessas than we realize. All right, give her weapons; I'll keep an eye on her."

Hal grinned and reached for his comm. "Ensign White to security officer Rhonda."

"Rhonda here, Hal, what's up?"

"You on the ship?"

"Yes."

"Bring me a weapons belt, size female small, dagger, blaster, baton, and flashlight only, no projectile weapon."

"Got it. Be right there."

A few moments later a female security officer came trotting over to them. She handed the belt to Hal then returned to her post aboard the ship. He looked around and finally spotted Sessas patrolling along the nearest wall. "Sessas." Nothing happened.

"Let me," grinned Twenty. She whistled a merry tune and Sessas instantly responded. At Twenty's signal she hurried over to them. She looked bewildered for a moment as Hal put the belt around her waist.

She squeaked with delight as she realized what it was. She paid close attention as Hal demonstrated the flashlight and baton. When he finished she hugged him tightly, pulled him down so she could touch her muzzle to his head, the hurried back to her patrol, the baton in her hand. Twenty winked at him then joined her, war hammer in hand. With a sigh and a chuckle, he followed.

Chapter 13

Of Ships and Fleets

A couple of weeks passed, and the salvage operation was nearly complete. The lizard men were keeping an eye on them but staying well back. The sight of a heavily armed Sessas was keeping them respectful. The small scout ships located three more mining operations on the planet, but none of them turned up anything useful.

Finally, the Admiral called a full staff meeting to discuss the situation. She paced about the briefing room as she waited for them to assemble. "All here and clear, Admiral."

Chuckling, Jeannie took her seat. "Thank you, First Officer. It's time for us to take a good look at where we stand, people. Let's start with Engineering. Moira?"

"Ah, Jeannie, I haven't had this much fun in years. We have, or soon will have, enough material to build three new Explorers. Explorer #2 is well under way. We've worked up full schematics for the ships, including Earalithian style weapons and energy shields. Ex #2 will be more than just an explorer ship; she'll be a lot tougher and fully capable of intense combat if required.

"Ex #2 will be twenty percent larger than the original with slightly more comfortable crew quarters for expected long absences from Reacher, and more powerful engines. She'll also have better sensors and stronger comm boosters. Ex #3 and #4 will be the same."

"Wow, I'm impressed, Moira. May I ask, why the sudden focus on weapons?"

"Dorind's idea, Jeannie. He says better to prepare for the worst and hope for the best. If Explorer One had better weapons she could have fought off those creatures and brought all her people home in one piece."

"I have to agree with the reasoning, we've faced old defense weapons, hostile animals and more. Who knows what we'll face in the days to come. Well done, Moira.

"Captain Volkov, how's the salvage operation going?"

"We've got most of the metal out of the main storage area, but Dorind's found us another smaller one full to the brim. We figured we might as well take that as well."

"Works for me. Captain Baris, how's the new ship working out?"

"Ah Jeannie, I'm having fun. We've got a small crew of hard-working people, we've made three trips with full holds so far, and I get to poke around on the planet while the lads do the work."

"How's Mr. Morita working out as First Officer?"

"The man's tireless, Jeannie. He recruited the crew, trained a few of them on salvage, helped design a few new tools to make the work easier, and more."

"So, you're happy?"

"I am."

"Then so am I. Captain Drake, how's Friendship Two working for you?"

"He's a great little ship, Admiral," smiled Amanda, "but we're a bit cramped. He was built for folk of a smaller stature. Linsey and Eighteen are fine on an Earalithian ship as they're both under five foot four. I'm five-eight and many of my crew are taller.

"Having said that, he's a tough and quick little ship. I'm encouraging Moira to incorporate a number of his features in the new ships."

"Excellent. Security?"

Sheila Singh sighed and sat up straighter to deliver her report. "Things on the Reacher are quiet, Admiral."

"But not so much on the surface?"

"Not so much. Early on in the salvage operation there was an incident."

"Oh?" Jeannie was grinning as she knew all about that.

"Yes. The lizard men reappeared and brandished their weapons. The leader used sign language to demand that SUVI 20 come to him."

"Oh, what happened?"

"You know dang well what happened, Suvi-jean. Sessas snatched a blaster from one of the security men and sent the lizard man flying. She then told the rest of the, in her words, assholes, to bugger off. They did, then Ensign Hal White requisitioned a weapons belt and strapped it on Sessas. She's been leading the security team ever since with SUVI 20 as her second.

"Between Sessas with her blaster and Twenty with her war hammer, they've effectively kept the lizard men at bay.

"Meanwhile, Jake took it upon himself to approach our armorer about some possible upgrades. What they came up with has both surprised and thrilled me. Had Jake been wearing this gear when he was carried off, he'd have had far fewer injuries to deal with. He's now commissioned a full refit for all our security forces."

"You believe this to be wise?"

"I do, Admiral, truly I do. If we'd had this armor when the ship was invaded, we'd have lost far fewer people and taken fewer injuries. This stuff's not pretty, but it sure is effective."

"That sounds like personal experience."

Sheila laughed at that. "It is, Jeannie. I put on a suit, took a few shots from a side arm, a few hard punches from Marcus, then deliberately fell out of the scaffolding in the cargo bay. Not a scratch on me."

Jeannie matched her grin. "Are you sure Marcus was trying?"

"He got into it after I decked him. In the end I had to suck up and talk the chef into making his favorite dessert. We're all good now."

"Awesome. Alien relations?"

"Me? Oh, yes, well, not a lot for me to do once we checked out the other mining operations. I've been working with Sessas every chance I get, but it's hard to pry her away from her self-appointed security job.

"It was Hal who gave me the clue. Sessas is naturally inquisitive, and has a loving nature, but it was a mistake to think of her as a child. She is a fully matured female, was captured in a raid by a rival clan, then abused badly when she was unable to produce enough eggs to satisfy the chieftain of the new clan.

"That one, an abusive brute, spotted SUVI 20 and decided to trade Sessas for her. It seems no one has ever said no to this guy before, and he doesn't like it. The fact that Sessas, a female, has faced and defeated him will hold them at bay for now, but she believes he will continue to try to acquire Twenty as a concubine."

"So, our girl is expecting trouble, is she?"

"She is, Admiral."

"I can see it in your eyes, Linsey, there's more."

"Yes, there is. Sessas is asking for more weapons. She wants to arm all the female slaves and lead them in an uprising against the asshole, as she's named him. Oh, she now fully understands the meaning of the word, but refuses to change it."

"I can't say I blame her for that. I'm not sure about giving her more weapons though. What do you think, people? Opinions? Options?"

It was her grandfather who first spoke up. "We can't give her weapons."

"Why not?"

"Jeannie, we have no right to interfere, we have no right to change the way their society is evolving."

"No right? No right to help a slave free her people? Is this not exactly what you did for me?"

"That was different."

"How so?"

Frank Baris sputtered and waved his hands in the air for a moment then started to chuckle. "I don't know, Jeannie, I don't. Maybe it's no different at all. We've met a member of an alien society who has aided us every chance she's had. Perhaps we're honor bound to help her in return. I don't know."

Jeannie smiled and reached out to lightly pat his hand. "Anybody else?"

"What weapons does she want, Linsey?" asked Sheila Singh.

"Six blasters and a dozen batons. She also wanted someone to teach her how to use the baton effectively. Hal has already started her training. He's teaching Sessas and SUVI 20 hand-to-hand fighting as well as small arms tactics. What do you think, Jeannie?"

"I want to talk to her first, but I'm inclined to give her the weapons. Okay, moving on. Second Officer?"

"All quiet on the bridge, Admiral. The new pilot in training is doing fine."

"New pilot?"

"We needed another pilot since Commander da Silva stole our last one," he grinned.

"So I see. Good then. Medical research?"

"Not a lot for me to report, Admiral, unless you're ready to discuss those embryos I've got in storage."

"Let's save that discussion until the next time we're interstellar and bored, shall we?" Everyone chuckled at that. "Medical?" Silence. "Carla?"

"Huh? Oh, yes, me, well we've had a few bumps and bruises from the salvage crews, a few strains and sprains, but nothing major. Jake and Twenty are back in action, so we're all good in Medical."

Jeannie gave her a sad look then went on. "All right then, is there anything from the passengers, Miriam?"

"There's a clamor for jobs on the ship building crews, plus the applications for crew positions on the smaller ships are piling up on Brandon's desk I'm sure.

"Admiral, things have changed since the last time you spoke directly to the passengers. Now the big excitement is the new ships, possible jobs, and a general sigh of relief from us older folk that we can actually retire in comfort. Retirement aboard the Reacher is a lot sweeter than it would be in the caverns of Elysium."

"Oh, what was that like?" asked Linsey.

"A quick trip to the surface to survive as best you could," replied Miriam.

"Oh. Sorry."

Jeannie chuckled then went on. "Okay, that's all good. Is there anything else for today? No? All right, meeting adjourned. Carla, a word in private. Mandy, stay please."

The others filed out leaving them alone. Jeannie reached out to take Carla by the hand. "What is it, dear friend? You've been lost in thought for days."

"Yeah, and cranky too. I'm sorry, Jeannie; I'll get over myself and do better."

"Jeannie wasn't chastising you, honey, she's worried about you. So am I." As she spoke, Amanda reached for Carla's other hand and gave it a gentle squeeze.

With a deep sigh, Carla returned the pressure on her hands then relaxed back in her chair. "Okay, I'll talk. It's Jake. He's distracted all the time, and I know he's thinking about her."

"SUVI 20?"

"Yes, Jeannie, your golden child has stolen my man."

Amanda leaned closer to take Carla's hand again. "Honey, I don't believe that for a minute. You told me they both swore nothing happened between them down there."

"I know, Mandy. I know. Maybe they didn't actually do anything, but they wanted to. I'm no fool, I can tell. The thing is, when he does come home, he holds me close, and I know he still loves me, he does, but she's still on his mind."

"When he comes home? I don't understand, where does he go?" asked Jeannie.

"I don't know, security office, the armory, maybe he wanders around. He won't talk about it, I've tried."

"Carla, I don't believe he's spending time with Twenty. He can't be, she's on the planet, he's here on the Reacher."

"I know, Jeannie. She's spending all her time on the planet with Hal and Sessas, patrolling. They say her mood is pretty blue too."

Jeannie sighed and sat back. "I know what's going on here. It's one of those human relationship things that nobody understands, and a SUVI is caught up in it. Obviously, they developed feelings for each other, but Jake had already given you his promise. He would never break that.

"Twenty also knows both you and Jake are highly placed in the crew of the Reacher. She would also hold herself back from him so as not to cause trouble for either of you."

"For the greater good?"

"Yes Carla, for the greater good."

"That's all well and fine, it defines the problem, but offers no solution. Any ideas?"

Amanda gave her hand another friendly squeeze. "Honey, what do you want to happen here? What outcome would you like to see?"

"Me? I want my life back; I want Jake back. The old Jake, nosey, teasing, gentle, loving, and ... I guess that can't ever happen now, can it? Just as Tara Reilly died long before Dr. Reilly woke her up and infected her with the virus, my Jake died of his injuries on an alien planet, and SUVI 20 brought him back to life, but he's not the same.

"Just like Tara's not the same, Jake's not the same. Whatever happened on that planet made her a permanent part of his life. Now she's withdrawn from him, and he's all messed up. From what I hear, so's she, and sadly, so am I."

"Carla ..."

"No, Mandy, it can't go back to the way it was. That time of innocence for us is gone." With that, she rose and left the briefing room.

While Carla was talking to Jeannie and Amanda, Jake was in the exercise area, wearing the new armor and facing off against SUVI 19. He landed several swift blows, but the big man shrugged them off then retaliated. Jake took a couple of hard hits and was sent sprawling.

Nineteen extended a hand to help him up. "Are you all right, Jake?"

"Yeah, I am, Nineteen. This armor really absorbs the hard hits. You saw how it took that jump of two levels yesterday. I'm really liking this stuff. Thanks for helping out."

"A pleasure. It's not often I can use my full strength or test myself."

"I believe that," grinned Jake, as he pulled off the armor. "I'll have a few bruises from this session, but it was close to what I fought on the planet. This time, no real injury. Can I ask you something?"

"Of course."

"I know you were First Prime's enforcer, but I get the sense it wasn't your idea."

"No, it wasn't."

"What was your job, before you got infected?"

Nineteen grinned. "I had your job, security man. I was a raw recruit when the call came out for security people to join the colonies. I thought it would be exciting."

"Be careful what you wish for."

"Indeed so. I didn't meet Farouk Bladon until we were boarding the ship to leave Earth. I knew instantly he was the wrong man for the job, but he was assigned to lead our contingent. There was nothing I could do.

"We were on Elysium only days when the Oraks came through. Farouk was the first to survive. It wasn't until two more survivors arrived that he suddenly took command and enslaved the SUVI. Facing as many weapons as he had at his command, we complied and were placed in the pain collars. I vowed to kill him if I could. My opportunity was a long time coming."

"Yeah, that had to be harsh. I can't even imagine."

"And that's a good thing. It means you'll never be like Farouk, even after you rise to the command of all security forces."

"Commander Singh is Chief of Security, Nineteen."

"She is, and she has over thirty years on you. You're the next in line, your fate is inevitable."

Jake grinned. "You make it sound like so much fun."

"Until your recent adventure on the planet, you thought so too."

"Yeah, that took the good out of me."

"Pain of the heart can be worse than pain of the body, my friend."

"Nineteen?"

"Jake, you're obviously in love with two women, one human, and one SUVI. The only way that could get worse is if you added an Earalith girl to the mix."

"Thanks, Nineteen, you're a big help. Any other useful suggestions?"

"Jake, I can't tell you what to do here, I can only tell you to look to the greater good when you do decide to take action."

Jake stopped walking and turned to fully face the huge SUVI. "That's what I'm trying to do, but it sure as hell isn't easy."

"It never is," replied Nineteen, as he lightly slapped Jake's shoulder. "Come, let's go to the mess grab some food."

"When all else fails, eat?"

"Absolutely."

Chapter 14

Trouble

J eannie sat in the captain's briefing room, staring off into space, her eyes glowing amber. Amanda found her there and gently tapped on the door. "Jeannie?"

"Huh? Oh hi, Mandy, come on in."

"Jeannie, are you hiding out in here?"

Suvi-jean chuckled at that. "No, Mandy, but I have been tempted to from time to time. No, I'm getting a bad feeling about that planet below. I fear it isn't finished causing us trouble."

"Have you checked in with Thirteen and Eighteen about this?"

"Not yet, but I'm thinking I should." She reached for her comm. "SUVI 13 and SUVI 18 to the bridge."

It was only moments when Thirteen arrived. "So you've felt it too, Five?"

"Any idea what's going on, Thirteen?"

"None, but I don't like this, not one bit."

"Nor do I. Where the heck is Eighteen? Computer, locate SUVI 18."

"SUVI 18 is no longer aboard Reacher. She departed on Friendship One."

"Dammit, this isn't good," said Jeannie, as she rose to her feet. "Come on." She marched out with Amanda and Thirteen close behind.

"Admiral on the bridge."

"As you were people. Emmet, do we have ships on the planet?"

"We do, Admiral. Recovery Two went down for the last load of salvage, but a storm came out of nowhere. Friendship One took a load of food and medical supplies down just in case, but this storm is a bad one. Friendship made it into the hangar, barely. Captain Baris ordered the bay doors closed, so until the storm abates, they're trapped down there."

"And so it begins," sighed Jeannie. "Call the senior staff to the briefing room, Emmet." She turned and walked away as the announcement went out over the ship's public address system. A short time later, those still aboard Reacher were in the briefing room.

"All right, we have two ships trapped on the planet and a major storm as we speak. As far as I know both ships are safe within the underground hangar. This much I know. Can any of you add more information to this?"

The chief engineer spoke first. "There was another half load of metals down there, so Captain Baris took Recovery Two down to fetch it. Recovery One has remained on the ground with the security teams for the entire salvage operation. When they called in about the storm, Linsey took a load of food and whatnot down to them. I assume she was unable to return. That must be some wicked storm if Friendship can't get back out."

"You're telling me we have three ships trapped down there."

"Sadly, Admiral, that I am."

"Jake, where is Sheila?"

"On the surface. Marcus has been down there for quite a while, so she decided to go down and see the place for herself."

"Oh for the love of ..." Jeannie was on her feet pacing now, her eyes glowing amber.

"There's more bad news."

"Spill it, Jake, all of it."

"I talked to Hal just before the storm hit. They've been seeing a lot more lizard activity, Sessas is getting nervous. I recommend we transport more security troops down just in case."

Jeannie sighed and resumed her seat. "We can't Jake. There's something in the atmosphere down there that messes with the comms, especially during the storms. I won't risk any lives on the transporter."

"Worried about your girlfriend, Jake?"

Jake turned to Carla, and with true sadness in his voice, answered her question. "Yes, I am, Carla. SUVI 20 saved my life a dozen times over, she's special to me. Sessas also saved my hide and helped us survive; she too is precious to me. My brother Hal is there, he's been a good friend to you your entire life.

"Commander Singh is down there. The woman is amazing, and I can learn so much from her; I want her to be safe. Jeannie's grandfather is there ..."

"All right, Jake, I get it. I'm sorry, you're absolutely right, and I am sorry." He nodded and reached for her hand and gave it a gentle squeeze.

"Okay people, recommendations? Options? Opinions?"

"We can't send people through the transporters, but could we send objects?"

"Brandon?"

"You know, some of Jake's new battle armor. Nineteen says it can take a serious pounding and the wearer is unharmed."

"How would he know that?"

"Sorry, Little Sister, but I talked Nineteen into beating me up, me in the suit. He's right, it'll take a serious pounding."

"All right, send some down, see if it works."

"With your permission, I'll get right to it."

"Go, Jake, then report back to me."

"Jeannie?"

"I don't want you to go crazy and risk the transporter yourself. Send it then come back and report."

He looked at her for a long moment. "I swear I'll come right back." She nodded and he hurried from the room.

"Brandon, please tell me we're good here in space."

He chuckled at that. "Yes, Admiral, we're good here. I spend my days fussing over details that don't really matter, Emmet paces around the bridge because he's bored, Eamon hides in his lab, probably reading old romance novels, Moira's the only one having any fun at all."

That finally brought a smile to Jeannie's face. "Tell me about it, Moira."

"Well, Explorer #2 is nearly ready for test flights. I could probably work faster without Captain Drake constantly peeking over my shoulder."

Amanda grinned at Moira's teasing remark. "What? I'm excited about the new ship, I can't help it."

Finally Jeannie smiled and relaxed. "How about the rest of them, Moira?"

"We're focusing on Ex #2, trying to get Amanda and crew back into space, but the hulls for #3 and #4 are nearly complete. We've been able to fabricate everything else we need, but it left us low on materials. That's why I asked Frank to go scrounge up the last of it. It's a lot easier to work with ready-made sheet metals than to mine and process it."

"Understood. Perhaps I'm fretting unnecessarily."

SUVI 13 had sat quietly at the end of the table while the meeting progressed. Now he spoke up. "You're not, Admiral. Jake's coming back."

At that moment Jake reentered the room and resumed his seat. "Jake, report."

"You were right about the transporters, Jeannie. I sent down twenty suits of armor, ten female and ten male. The suit will mold to your body if you get a rough fit. Anyway, four female and one male arrived intact, three more were shredded, and the rest went god knows where. We don't dare try to send anything more through."

"Then we shall hope it was enough. Jake, give us your assessment of the lizard men, how much of a threat could they pose?"

"Hard to say. They're fast like a SUVI, but no stronger than a human, their spears are crude, but could still cause a fatal wound if they hit the right spot. I've only encountered them in small groups, five or six at a time, but if they came in force they could be trouble."

"As acting Chief of Security, what do you recommend?"

"Commander Singh is there, and with Hal to back her up, a few people in the new armor, I'm confident they can handle the situation, if there actually is one developing. They're going to have to, because we can't do anything to help them.

"I've got to say, this really sucks. It was easier being in the thick of things than it is waiting and worrying."

"I agree with you there, big brother. Ah well, we'll trust them to deal with whatever comes their way. Moira, is there any chance that ship can be ready sooner?"

"Aye, Jeannie. I'll put an extra crew on it right now." The admiral nodded; the Chief Engineer fled the room, issuing orders over the comm as she went.

"I guess that's it then. Meeting adjourned, unless anyone has anything else." There was nothing, so the room quickly emptied out; leaving Amanda trying to keep Jeannie from fretting.

As they left the briefing room, Carla reached for Jake's hand. "Honey, I'm truly sorry. I embarrassed you in there and ..."

"It's okay, sweetheart, honestly, it's okay. I know I've put you through hell these past few weeks. I need to get my head straight. I'll do better, I promise."

Carla stopped walking and pulled him around to face her. "No, Jake, I'm the one who has to do better, get my head straight. I need to find Antha." With that she released his hand and walked away, leaving him wondering what the hell had just happened.

WHILE JEANNIE WAS HOLDING her staff meeting, things were getting a bit tense down on the planet. "I don't like this, Olga. What do you think?"

"I agree, Frank. Neither one of us is a combat officer, actually I don't know if anyone here has any combat experience at all."

"Actually, they do. Hal White is here, a veteran of the grounder invasion, and Sheila Singh as well."

"In that case I think we should call them in for a conference." She reached for her comm. "Ensign Hal White and Commander Singh to Recovery One. Repeat, Ensign Hal White and Commander Sheila Singh to Recovery One."

"On our way, Captain."

A few moments later they arrived together. "Captain Volkov, you wanted to see us?"

"Yes, Sheila. Frank and I agree that things aren't looking too good here, but neither of us has any combat experience. We're also old enough to know just taking charge and issuing orders isn't the best way to go about this.

"Sheila, it looks like we could be headed for trouble with the lizard men. Take charge here, tell us what you need."

Just then a crewman stuck his head through the door. "Excuse me, Captain, but we just got a shipment from the Reacher."

"The Reacher? They used the transporters?"

"Yes, ma'am. They sent security armor, twenty suits. Four female and one male arrived intact, three more completely shredded, and I have no idea what happened to the rest."

"Those were the new super suits?"

"Yes, Commander Singh."

"Thank you, Crewman. Hal, you decide who wears the new armor, you've been down here the longest."

Hal nodded. "You, me, SUVI 20, Sessas, and Officer Rhonda Moore in the new armor would be my choice."

"Make it happen, Hal. If they attack, we take the front with the rest of our people on the second line in traditional armor."

Hal hurried away to organize the armor and to help Twenty get Sessas into hers. He also enlisted Linsey's help to reassure Sessas this was a good thing.

While they were getting Sessas armored and showing her how it all worked, Commander Singh was still working with the other captains.

She also sent for Linsey, but it was Eighteen who arrived. "Forgive me, Commander Singh, but Linsey is helping Hal convince Sessas the armor is safe and a helpful thing. Can I be of service?"

"You'll do just fine, Eighteen. In fact, I was just about to call for you. What can you tell us about the situation with the lizard men? Are we facing an attack?"

"Yes, I believe we are. I had hoped we would be finished and gone before they fully organized, but the storm has prevented that. They aren't ready yet, but I sense them gathering, working up their courage."

"Your best guess, Eighteen, how soon?"

"Two days, Commander, but that's just a guess. There's no way I can tell for sure."

"That's a lot better than I had a right to expect. Thank you, Eighteen. Now, here's the plan. The salvage work is done. The captains are pulling their crews back to the ships.

"I highly doubt the lizard men can do any damage to a ship, but I'd rather they not get that opportunity. Security forces will form and defend a tight perimeter around the ships. You have no combat troops, so keep the crew of Friendship inside."

"Understood, Commander." SUVI 18 nodded, then left to gather Linsey and the crew back at the ship.

Outside, Sheila joined Hal and company, he and Rhonda were working with Twenty and Sessas as they got used to the armor. Sessas was fussing because it made her tail bunch up. Twenty was trying not to laugh and failing. This wasn't going to be easy.

It took the rest of the day, but Sessas began to see the advantages of the armor. Twenty grasped it instantly. "Jake invented this?"

Sheila chuckled at that. "Not actually invented, our armorer Harlan had been secretly working on this for years, he was bored. Jake went to him and asked for better armor and between them they came up with this.

"I've tried it out and I have to say, it will take quite a pounding. Now, Sessas, if they attack, which way will they come from?"

The Saurian girl gazed at her with big unblinking eyes. She'd understood her name, but nothing else. Twenty laughed and joined the conversation. "Sessas. Assholes, where?"

She used more body language than sound, and the girl instantly understood. "Assholes, Tentee." She swept her arm out to indicate the far reaches of the bay, then turned and pointed to the left wall as well. She began to wiggle the three fingers of her left hand. "Maneeeasssholesss."

"Understood, little sister," smiled Twenty, as she hugged the girl and kissed the top of her head. "She says …"

"Got it," grinned Commander Singh. "The assholes will come from there and there."

"Yes, she says there's a lot of them."

"Then we'd best prepare for visitors. Hal, your recommendations?"

"Well, Linsey's gunner is a real sharpshooter. If we could turn Friendship around a bit, he could cover our left flank from inside the ship."

"And that would leave us free to focus our forces on the main tunnel. I'll go talk to Linsey right now. You three pull your traditional patrols back closer to the ships, we've got all the salvage we're going to get from this place. The key now is to get out of here in one piece."

"Any idea how long the storm will last, Commander?"

"SUVI 18's best guess is three more days. I get the impression we'll have company before that." With that, she turned and headed for Friendship.

Linsey was at the hatch to greet her as Commander Singh reached Friendship. "Welcome aboard, Commander."

"Thank you, Captain da Silva. Wow, this is one cozy ship."

"Call me Linsey, please. Yes, Ship was built for Earalith sized folk like you and me."

"I can see that. Linsey, Hal says you've got a sharpshooter on your ship."

"Sure do. Mendalo can do amazing things with the weapons. What do you need?"

"Sessas believes we could face an attack on two fronts, the main tunnel and the left wall. We know there are several tunnels there made by the Saurians. Is there any way you can turn your ship to cover that wall? It would give us a big advantage."

"I'm not sure, Ettelan?"

"I can put us in position easily, Captain Linsey. Mendalo, what do you need?"

"Three or four degrees hard left should do, Ettelan." The ship rose slightly, turned, then settled back down. "That's perfect. I can cover the whole wall from here, Captain Linsey. We have plenty of ammunition. I'll set the proximity sensors to alert me if we have enemies approaching."

"Thank you, Mendalo, Ettelan. All set, Commander Singh."

"Sheila, call me Sheila, Linsey. Thank you."

"I just don't really understand, if they only use spears for weapons, are they truly that great a threat?"

"One on one, no, but in huge numbers they could easily overwhelm us. On top of that, I'm told they offered Sessas in trade because she couldn't lay enough eggs? Try to imagine the fate one of us would face if we were captured."

"Right, none of our three species lays eggs. I see your point, that's funny and nasty all at the same time. Okay, we've got the wall."

WHILE SESSAS WAS LEARNING to wear armor, Carla sought out Antha. She had finally set up a small office near Linsey's. "Come in, Commander Marks, welcome."

"Hi, Antha."

"Oh dear, someone carries a heavy load today."

"I do, I let my jealousy run my mouth and embarrassed myself in a staff meeting. Worse, I embarrassed Jake."

Antha set down the tablet she'd been reading. "Tea?"

Carla nodded. "Please. So, enjoying your new office?"

"I am, Commander. It's so different here for me. As a woman of a lower class in the empire, I was never treated well, and was allowed little comfort for myself. Here on the Reacher, I'm treated with respect, have many friends, and have found I'm useful. I'm enjoying the luxury of it all.

"Now, stop trying to change the subject." She smiled warmly as she passed Carla a mug of Earalithian tea.

Carla took a sip and sighed with delight. "I'm already addicted to this stuff, so glad Lilly was able to get the right bushes and grow the berries for the tea."

"As am I, but you're avoiding again. Commander, if this is too fresh or painful to talk about, we truly can discuss the tea production."

Carla laughed and shook her head. "No, Antha, I've been avoiding this for weeks, I do need to talk." Antha didn't speak, just relaxed in her chair giving Carla her undivided attention. "I'm sure you're aware of the mess I'm in, with Jake and SUVI 20."

"Mess?"

"He's in love with her."

"But?"

"I still love the big lug, and I know he still loves me. I know this has to be some sort of SUVI thing; he can't help himself."

Antha smiled. "No man in love ever can."

That made Carla laugh. "Yeah, I guess not. The problem is I get jealous as hell."

"And you don't like that."

"No, I hate it when I do that. It's not as though he cheated on me, and he still loves me."

"But that's not enough?"

"What? No ... yes, I don't know. Antha, what are you saying here?"

"The jealousy is anger at having lost something important. What do you believe you've lost?"

Carla sighed and spoke so softly Antha could barely hear her. "Jake."

"You say he didn't betray your trust, his promise to you, and that he still loves you. I don't understand, what has been lost?"

"A piece of him. Even when he's with me a piece of him is still with her. Antha, please help me here. What am I going to do?"

"First you must decide what it is you truly want."

"I want Jake to be happy again."

"Is that all?"

"No, I want to be happy too."

"So, you want everything to go back to the way it was before he went down to the surface?"

"Yes."

"I know exactly how you feel, Commander."

"Antha?"

"All too often, I find myself wishing things could go back to the way they were on the colony, but that can never be. Commander, life events cause changes in things, people, in ways that cannot be undone. We can never go back to the way things were, we can only go forward.

"With that in mind, try to find a way to be happy yourself and perhaps that will make Jake happier too."

"Is that what you do, Antha?"

"It is. We can't go back, but we're here on this wonderful ship with new and interesting people. In the colony, my most cherished Morthel spent much of her time in the home, hiding from the rest of the people, working on her journal. Now she works on Explorer, has many friends there, and loves it. This has made her happier than she has ever been, and although I have less time in her company, I take great joy in that."

"Wow. So, you're saying you have less time with her, but because she's so much happier, so are you?"

"Yes. I wasn't at first, but it was the Admiral who gave me the key."

"Jeannie? How? What key?"

"The driving motivation of the SUVI, for the greater good. By trying to see my situation through the filter of the SUVI, I could see how much happier Morthel is, and how she has found a way to contribute to the greater good, I discovered I could take joy in that.

"I've lost nothing of her, for she's now greater than she was before. Yes, I have less time with her, but the time I do have is happier. I have come to love her stories of the banter between Captain Drake and SUVI 13."

At that point Carla's comm beeped. "Damn, duty calls. Antha, thank you, you've given me much to think about."

Antha smiled and nodded as Carla fled her office. "You have quite a puzzle before you, friend Carla. I hope you can find the solution."

Carla hurried into the medical bay to find several people getting bandaged up. "What do you need?"

"We've got this handled, Commander," replied one of the medics, "but we're not sure if there are more injured."

"What happened?"

"An explosion in the shipbuilding section of Engineering."

Carla grabbed her comm unit. "Medical to Engineering."

"Moira here, Carla, relax, you've got all the wounded. Was anybody seriously hurt?"

After a quick glance to her medic who shook his head no, she replied. "Doesn't look like it. What happened?"

"It's a complicated story, but the short version is, these new metals can be a bit cranky when being worked. Somebody partied too much last night, got sloppy this morning, and bang. Overtired and distracted people make mistakes. I doubt it will happen again."

"Okay, thanks. Are you sure we've got all the walking wounded?"

"You do."

"Okay then, as soon as they're patched up we'll send them back to you. Medical out." She turned back to the busy medic. "So, Harry, what have we got?"

"A few bumps and bruises, a few surface wounds, and a lot of headaches from the concussion of the explosion. Two of these lads should go home and get a day off, the rest can go back to work."

"All right, Harry, you've got this. I'll be in the office."

"You okay, Commander?"

"Yeah, I'm good."

"You had me fooled," he muttered quietly, as she closed her office door.

Inside the office, Carla sank into her chair, rested her chin in her hands, and sighed. "Moira's right, overtired and distracted people make mistakes. My stellar performance in the staff meeting this morning will testify to that. For some reason, I believe Antha gave me the key to this thing, for the greater good.

"Okay, with that in mind, applying it to the current situation, how and where does it apply? All right, Twenty wants Jake, but he's married. Jake falls for Twenty, but he's married, so he can't act on that desire. Anybody else might, but not Jake. No, he'll stick to his promise even if it makes him miserable for the rest of his life.

"Now about SUVI 20, she falls for Jake, but knows she can't have him. She flirts with him because she can't help herself. She's the first SUVI to ever experience this because she's the first one without the experiences of slavery to shut it off. So, what does that mean?

"Something happened on that planet to throw them together, gave her the need to care for and nurture him, making that desire stronger for them both. However, Jake being Jake, and she, being SUVI, they agree to hold themselves apart for the greater good.

"The greater good? Right, he has status on the ship, I have status on the ship, she'll pull back to keep from disrupting the command structure of the home ship, the leaders of the herd. Makes sense, I guess, but it's not working. I'm upset, unhappy, distracted, and making mistakes.

"So is Jake. Jeannie was actually afraid he would try to transport himself down there today. That tells me just how protective he is of Twenty. Otherwise, he would be confident in Hal's ability to handle the situation.

"Now that brings us to the crux of the matter, it's not working. Both of them are working for the greater good of the herd, but it isn't working. Why not?"

Here she sighed and leaned back in the chair as it suddenly became clear to her. "It's not working because I'm not, not working for the greater good. I'm just being jealous, afraid, and messing things up for everybody. Jake's unhappy, Twenty's unhappy, Jeannie and Manda are worried about me and Jake, Jeannie is worried about Twenty, and I'm the root of the problem."

Again she sighed deeply. It's never easy to admit you're wrong, or that you're behaving badly, but she had to face it. Her jealousy was causing a lot of trouble for everybody, including herself. "All right, just what is it I want here? I'm the unhappiest of them all, and I hate that. I want to be happy again, I want Jake to be happy, and I want my friends to be happy and not to be worrying about me.

"So, how do I get back to happy again? Antha says to look at the situation through the filter of the SUVI mantra, for the greater good. What can I do to change this thing? Jake and Twenty are trying to do this for the greater good but failing because I'm not helping. How can I help them stay apart and lessen their feelings for each other?

"I can't. I've been in love with Jake all my life. I've tried to lessen that, to dampen it down a hundred times and failed every time. So, what's left?" She sat lost in thought for some time, then the solution came to her. "Oh, hell no. Really? Seriously? Carla Jean Marks, are you seriously thinking this?" she asked herself aloud.

She sighed. "It truly is the only answer I can see. All right, how the heck would that work? I'd have to ..."

Chapter #15

Showdown

The sleep cycle passed and no alarms sounded, night shift crews reported all quiet, but neither SUVI could offer any hope that it might last. Eighteen and Twenty stood side by side near Friendship watching Hal and Sessas pace along the defensive barricade made of empty ingot crates. "Eighteen ..."

"I know. I can feel them out there too."

"You should go back into the ship, I'm the warrior here."

"I have faced hardship and struggle before, my sister. I can stand at your side."

Twenty turned and gave her a gentle hug. "I know you can, but I have the armor and I've faced these things before. Please go back to Linsey and keep her safe."

"Twenty, he is safe too, and so is Linsey."

"Eighteen?"

A small grin touched Eighteen's lips. "Who do you think you're talking to here?"

"Can't hide anything from you, can I?"

"No, my sister, you can't. I feel the love in you, and I feel your pain at having to push it aside." She reached out to squeeze Twenty's arm. "This will not last forever, I promise. Put it aside now and focus, the assholes are coming." With that she patted Twenty's arm and turned back to the ship.

SUVI 20 shook off the mood and settled the helmet on her head. Stepping up to Sessas and Hal, she took the hammer from her belt and spoke softly. "Get ready, folks, they're coming."

Hal nodded and turned toward the ships as he reached for his comms. "Heads up, people. We've got company."

At that signal Sheila Singh donned her helmet and stepped out of the ship. "Lights!" The entire bay was suddenly flooded with strong light from the ships. Sessas had been warned and had been fitted with filters for her helmet. Her species spent their lives in the darkness or dimly lit corridors of the vast mining complex. The light would hurt their eyes.

As the lights came up they saw the entire bay filled with Saurian spearmen. Row after row of them stood staring back at the spaceships and the few defenders facing them. One large one stepped forward and pointed at the ground beside him. "There's the asshole," muttered Twenty.

"Assshole," agreed Sessas. Without warning she stepped out to face him, saying something in their own language.

At the sight of Sessas stepping out, both Linsey and Eighteen came running. Eighteen was carrying a big scatter blaster. Linsey stopped beside Sheila and stared intently at Sessas and the big lizard man. "Linsey, what the hell is she saying?"

"Not exactly sure, Commander, but I think she trying to explain to them all that Twenty belongs to Jake and can't lay eggs anyway. She's calling him something nasty, I think stupid asshole might be a close translation."

"Great. That's helpful."

"Maybe I should talk to them. I ..."

"Will stay back behind me," said Eighteen. Her tone left no room for argument. "You're too important to the people of the Reacher to risk. Stay back, and at the first sign of trouble return to the ship."

Linsey sighed and nodded. "Yes dear, I hear and obey. Oh shit."

"Linsey?"

"Sessas is telling the females at the back to turn on the males, to rise up, to demand to be free, equals. Look, there's one coming forward."

A large female came right up to Sessas, gently and respectfully working her way through the mass of spear carriers. They faced off for a moment then she spoke. Sessas responded. The conversation went on for a while, then Sessas turned away, her shoulders slumping. She went straight to Twenty and snuggled into her arms, her body trembling.

As they watched the large female return through the crowd, Twenty spoke. "Linsey, what the hell just happened?"

"It was a bit too fast for me to follow, but I'll give it a shot. Sessas asked the females to revolt, but they refused. She told them about life on the Reacher, how everybody is equal, everybody is respected. They don't care.

"That big one was the lead female from her old clan, the one she was captured from. They don't want her back, they just want us gone, but the leader won't let us go until he gets you. Sessas told him you can't lay eggs, but they don't believe her. They think she's crazy, that we're controlling her mind. If she tries to go back to them she'll be killed.

"I could be wrong, but that's my best guess."

"Son of a bitch."

Sheila Singh stepped closer. "So what happens now?"

"Now we take Sessas with us," declared Twenty.

"Absolutely, but that's not what I meant."

"I guess they won't back off until that jerk gets his prize. Might as well give him what he wants."

"Twenty, what the hell are you doing?"

"Giving him what he wants."

The big saurian was insistently pointing to the ground beside him. Twenty shed her armor then stepped toward him. "Twenty ..."

"Back off, all of you, this is personal." She walked meekly toward the spearman until she was close enough, then she struck. He had no time to react as, with a scream of primal fury, she leaped at him, swinging the war hammer. It struck his skull, shattering it, blood spraying everywhere.

Twenty kicked aside the body and spat on it. "Asshole." Nobody moved as she walked back and pulled on the armor once again. As soon as she was ready, she faced the horde of spearmen and pulled Sessas close to her side, kissed the top of her head, then stood defiantly facing the wall of spears.

"Well, looks like the negotiations are over," muttered Hal.

"Apparently," agreed Sheila. "Brace yourselves people, this could get ugly and fast."

It didn't though. After a long wait, and not a single Saurian moving a muscle to leave or attack, they began to get nervous. "Linsey, ask Sessas what the hell is going on now?"

Linsey spoke to Sessas who barely responded. She weakly waved her arm at the horde and hissed a soft, "Asssholesss."

Linsey tried again, and this time got more of a response. She turned back to Commander Singh. "She says they're waiting."

"For?"

"Us to leave, or to fight them. Twenty killed the leader of that small clan, he was the leader, so now perhaps she can take over."

"What? Me?"

"It's worth a shot," grinned Hal.

"Sure, what the hell. Nothing to lose by giving it a try," agreed Twenty. She passed Sessas to Hal's arms then took a few steps toward the throng of spearmen. Slowly she raised her arm and pointed to the tunnels. "Go!"

Nothing happened. She tried again, still nothing. Sessas stepped up beside her and spoke to the throng. Slowly they lowered their spears and began to withdraw. At length, only one small clan was left.

The female who had first spoken with Sessas came to them. She spoke to Sessas, but Sessas waved her fingers dismissively and turned her back. The female rejoined her people and they disappeared into the tunnels.

Twenty turned to Linsey. "Linsey, what did she say to Sessas?"

"She told her to go away, they don't want her back. Sessas basically told her to piss off."

"Yeah, I got that part. So, it's over now?"

"Yes, Commander Singh, I believe it is, but we have a problem."

"What's that, Linsey?"

"Sessas. What's to become of her?"

"She comes with us," declared Twenty.

"Twenty, that's for the admiral to decide."

"We can't abandon her now ..."

"We won't, Twenty, we won't," soothed Linsey. "I'm in command of all alien relations, remember? For now, I say we keep her with us, and I'll recommend the same to the admiral the first chance I get."

"The SUVI will also champion her cause," agreed Eighteen. "We'll care for her, my sister."

Somewhat mollified, Twenty relaxed her arms about Sessas. "Well, I'm not ready to call this one a win until we're safely back in space. Come on, Sessas, we'll patrol the area."

"Yesss, pat rollll."

"Works for me," grinned Sheila. "Stay sharp, people. I'll go report in to the captains."

They kept the lights on all day, and the patrols went on, but the tunnels remained empty. At the end of shift, when nothing had happened, they dimmed the lights and set the proximity alarms. Deep in the night, the alarms sounded.

Everybody leaped from their beds and donned their armor or raced to their stations. The lights came up and once again the entire area was filled with lizard men carrying spears. "Well, crap, here we go again," muttered Hal.

"Second that," agreed Twenty, as she and Sessas appeared at his side. "Now what the hell is going on?"

"Beats me. Here comes Commander Singh and Linsey."

Sheila Singh arrived with Linsey and Eighteen. "What's the good word, Hal?"

"Don't know, Commander. They're just standing there like yesterday."

"Linsey?"

"Can't say, Commander. Nobody's talking over there, so... not much I can tell you until they do."

"Oh damn, looks like they've got a new leader," said Twenty. "He doesn't look friendly. Eighteen?"

"Agreed, he appears to be angry with us."

"Great," muttered Sheila, "and here I thought we were going to get out of here without any bloodshed. Can anyone ask him what he wants?"

"No, Commander. As I understand this, he's the leader and he gets to speak first. If we break that rule it could set them off."

"Okay fine then, we'll wait him out. Can somebody bring me some coffee?" One security officer behind her chuckled and turned back to Recovery Two. He soon returned with a container of steaming liquid. She groaned with delight as she took a long sip.

Sheila's coffee was long gone before the new leader stepped forward and lowered his spear, pointing at the ground before him. "Okay, looks like he wants to talk now."

"About bloody time," grumbled Sheila. "So, how do we do this?"

"Sessasssspppeak." With that she walked out to face the big spearman. There was a lot of hissing and posturing, but he showed no real aggression, keeping his spear pointed at the ground. Finally, she returned. "Asssholesayyy leave, no fight. Ssstaaay, fight. Sessas say storm, no leave. Ssstormssstop, leave. He sssayisss good."

Linsey took Sessas by the shoulders and gazed into her eyes. "What else did he say?"

"He sssayySessas no come back."

Linsey and Eighteen hugged her and kissed the top of her head. "Then you come with us, be part of the crew." Eighteen nodded her agreement. Together they led her into the ship. The new leader of the saurians watched her go and nodded his approval.

Commander Singh reached for her comm. "Captain Volkov, how's our weather doing out there, do you know?"

"Sensors say it's still bad, but we could make a run for it. What's going on?"

"Sessas worked out a deal with the lizard men. We leave and take her with us. Anything else will get ugly."

"All right then, we'll recall all personnel to the ships and give it a shot."

All personnel were soon back on the ships. The huge bay doors slid open to show the raging storm outside as the ships began to rise. Friendship went first and shot away toward open space. She was followed closely by Recovery One and Recovery Two. It was a struggle, but they made their way back off world and headed for the Reacher.

"ADMIRAL, THIS IS THE bridge."

"Let me finish breakfast before you give me bad news, Emmet."

"It's good news, Admiral. Three ships returning."

"I'll be in the arrivals area. Sorenson out." Jeannie jumped up, grabbed Amanda's hand, and headed for the cargo bay. Jake returned the platters and ran to join them. They found Carla waiting. "Carla, we've got injured coming?"

"Don't think so, Jeannie. I just thought I'd be here in case."

Jeannie chuckled softly. "Yes, the right woman for the job."

The big bay doors opened and Recovery Two swept in, moving as close to the far end as possible to off load her cargo. Recovery One landed close behind, and Friendship was last in then the doors closed behind him, and atmosphere was returned to the area. The isolation field dropped, and the hatches opened, spilling out happy returning crews.

Sessas spotted Jake and ran to him, throwing herself into his arms, talking in a language he couldn't understand. He smiled as he hugged her and kissed the top of her head.

Hal and Twenty were right behind her and Jake instantly noticed his grandfather's ring on a chain around Twenty's neck, it had fallen out of her shirt. "Hal gave it to me," she said defensively.

Jake looked at Hal who nodded. "Then it's found its proper home," sighed Jake. "You okay, Twenty?"

"Yeah, I'm good."

"I'll be the judge of that," said Carla, as she joined them. "Report to my office in an hour for a checkup."

"Seriously?"

"Seriously, sister. You be there. Hal, my office, now." Carla reached out and lightly flicked the ring that hung around Twenty's neck. Twenty blushed slightly and tucked it back under her shirt. Carla gave her a strange look then grabbed Hal and led him away.

Sessas took Twenty by the hand and pulled her closer to Jake. Reflexively he started to reach for her, but she put out a hand and stopped him. "Don't, Jake. It'll break me if you do."

He sighed deeply, nodded and let his hand fall away. "I'm glad you're alright. I was worried about you."

"Just me?" she asked, the old twinkle in her eye again.

Jake smiled in spite of himself. "Well no, I was worried about Sessas too, you know, gotta look out for my girls."

"So, I've still got my title?"

"You'll always have that, Twenty, you know that."

She gazed into his eyes for a moment then shook off the mood. "I think the admiral needs you."

He turned to look, but Jeannie was hugging her grandfather. He turned back, but Twenty was already gone. He sighed as he watched her walk away.

"CARLA, I'M FINE. WHAT'S going on?"

Carla closed her office door. "Hal, what happened down there? Come on, I saw the family ring on SUVI 20's neck. Talk to me old buddy."

"Carla, please, I don't want ..."

"Hal, you've been a friend, more like a brother, for all my life. Honey, I'm not asking you to get in the middle here, there's too many of us in here right now anyway. I just want to know how it got there."

"I gave it to her."

"Well I could have guessed that. I saw you wear it before you left. Talk or I'll give you a shot to make you talk."

Hal laughed at that. "All right, I'll talk. Please don't shoot me. I like SUVI 20, she's a good person. She was so damned unhappy, then she spotted me wearing the ring. She wanted to know why I had it, so I told her. She understood, but I broke down and gave it to her. That's all she can have of him, Carla, and we all know that. She knows that."

"I could be wrong, but I get the feeling that, for the SUVI, this emotional stuff is powerful, so I ..."

"Did the right thing, Hal. You did the right thing. So, what else happened down there? Did that big lizard come back for her?"

"Yeah, he did, and he brought hundreds of friends with him. Twenty cracked his skull with that war hammer of hers and they went away."

"Wow."

"Yeah. Scared the hell out of me when she did it. She took off the armor and walked out to him. He was smirking, pointing at the ground by his feet when she whipped out the hammer and splattered his brains all over the storage area. Problem solved."

"I repeat, wow." Just then the announcement came. " All senior staff to the bridge. All captains and passenger representatives to the bridge."

Chapter #16

Piecing it Together

"**A**ll requested personnel present, Admiral."

"Thank you, First Officer. All right, people, are we finished with this one? Captain Volkov?"

"I think we've got everything useful from that planet, Admiral."

"Captain Baris?"

"I agree, Jeannie. I'd say we're done with it."

"Alien relations?"

"Me?"

"You, Linsey. Is there anything more you have to do down there?"

"No, Admiral, but there is one issue. I'll defer that one to Social Engagement."

"Seriously? Mandy?"

"It's Sessas, we have to decide what to do with her."

"Do with her? I don't understand."

"Linsey can explain it better, she was there."

"Talk to me, Linsey."

"Yes Admiral. On the planet we were confronted by a large force of the Saurian people. Their leader was demanding we hand over SUVI 20. Sessas tried to talk sense to them, she failed. She tried to incite a revolt against him, again she failed.

"Sessas was originally abducted from her clan in a slave raid. By a stroke of fortune, she came to us. Sadly, it was made clear to her by her own people, especially her original clan, that they don't want her back. She was a slave, part of a fairly offered trade, and they all wanted

Twenty to comply and Sessas to go away. That's when Twenty brained the leader.

They went away to elect a new leader, then returned. Sessas talked to him, and he made it clear, she goes away and takes all the aliens with her, everything is good. If not, they'd attack and kill us all, so he said. The weather was clearing up a bit, so we chanced a lift off rather than destroy a whole species.

"They were using spears, Admiral, and we had the power of modern weapons, full armor, and ships with heavy weapons. We were ready to fight if we had no choice, but ..."

"No, Linsey, it was well done. So Sessas is still on the Reacher? Has anyone asked her what she wants to do?"

"I have, Admiral, but it wasn't in my power to grant, that's for Social Engagement or you to decide."

"What does she want to do, Linsey."

"In her words, Admiral, stay on the Reacher, help people, stay away from assholes."

Jeannie chuckled at that. "She doesn't want to go back to the planet. Have you explained we're going far away, never to return? She'll never again see one of her own kind."

"She understands, Admiral, but this girl had never known a kindness until Jake and Twenty defended her and adopted her. She sees them as her clan, family, and wants to stay with them."

"Then it's settled, she can stay with us. Mandy, you'll have to find her a job somewhere."

"Already done, Admiral," grinned Amanda. "All we needed was you're okay."

"You've got it. So, what's her job?"

"Security officer aboard Friendship," grinned Linsey. "She's good with weapons, cool headed in a situation, and has a strong sense of right and wrong."

"And you're the only one of us who can truly communicate with her. I like it, Linsey. You made a translation device for us to communicate with the Earalith, could you do the same for her?"

"It's a very different sort of language, Admiral, but I've got one in the works. With luck it'll work well enough."

"Then we're all good there. Security?"

"Linsey already gave you the meat of what happened down on the planet. We faced a horde of Saurians wielding spears. Sessas tried to negotiate but failed, then SUVI 20 negotiated a temporary truce. The next day we were told to take our sorry butts and get the hell off their planet. We did and here we are. There was only one casualty, the original leader of the saurians."

Jeannie chuckled. "So, Twenty tried a different style of negotiating?"

"She did, it was quite effective."

"All right then, Engineering, are you satisfied we're done here?"

"We are, Jeannie. There's nothing left down there worth fighting over. We've got everything we need to finish the new ships; EX #2 is nearly finished and Amanda is anxious to find someplace to explore so she can test it out."

"All right then. Medical?"

"We're good, Admiral. Everybody got out unscathed. We're good to go."

"Perfect, Second Officer, is there anything out there that looks interesting?"

Emmet Jones grinned with delight. "Aye, Admiral, there's a binary system nearby, about six weeks away. There seems to be a number of planets circling the twin stars. Might be worth a look."

"Then let's go take a look. First Officer, prepare the ship for interstellar travel. Second Officer, go back to the bridge and aim us at that system. Let me know when everything is ready for the jump."

"Aye, Admiral," grinned Emmet as he rose, saluted, then limped back to the main bridge."

"Miriam, I apologize, I just assumed the passengers wouldn't want to try colonizing that planet."

"You were absolutely correct, Admiral. That one was even less hospitable than Elysium. We'll pass on it happily."

Carla returned to the medical bay and found SUVI 20 waiting for her. "Reporting for inspection as ordered, Commander."

"Sit down, relax, Twenty. I'm not your enemy here."

"Sorry, I ..."

"Please, just listen. We need to talk, I need to talk, and I need you to listen. You didn't bring that hammer with you, did you?"

"What? No, it's in my quarters."

"Oh good. I've heard how you use that in negotiations."

That made Twenty laugh. "Yeah, I know I shouldn't have done that. I know it was wrong, but ..."

"You're frustrated and hurting, that asshole wouldn't take no for an answer, so he paid the price. I'd like to think I'd have done the same."

"Thanks for that. So, is that what we're doing here? Negotiating?"

"Sort of. Actually, let's call it figuring things out."

"I don't understand."

"Girl, I know damn well you've got a SUVI-sized case for my guy, that's easy to see. You and I both know he has a thing for you too. However, he still loves me, and I've loved him all my life, so, as you may gather, I'm somewhat unwilling to let him go."

"You don't have to let him go, Commander. You're married to him, and he'll never betray that, and as you say, he still loves you, so, I don't understand what's going on here. If you're telling me to stay away from him, I have been, and I will continue to do so."

"For the greater good?"

"Yes. Both you and Jake are vital to the well being of the people aboard the Reacher. I won't interfere with that."

"You see, there's the problem. You already are."

"Excuse me?"

"Relax, Twenty, put down the hammer. I'm not the enemy here, and neither are you. Twenty, I know you and Jake were just being playful here on the Reacher. I had no issues with that. However, something happened down on that planet to change things."

Twenty sighed and fairly melted back into her chair. "Yeah, can't argue that."

"Can you tell me how it happened for you?"

"Sure, why not. I had a strong sense he would get into trouble down there, so I tagged along. I saw him get carried off by that animal, so I didn't think, I just went after them. I found him in a falling down cave.

"He was in rough shape, so I patched him up a bit, then we settled down to wait out the storm. Jake recognized why I started to come unglued when the SUVI abandoned the planet. He held me so gently, kissed my noggin and told me to behave. As hurt as he was, his big concern was to keep me from freaking out.

"As we explored for food and better shelter, Jake fell through the roof of an old mining tunnel. We'd been separated and when I found the hole where he fell, I jumped in. It was a long fall for me, must have been hell for Jake, as hurt as he was.

"Anyway, it was pitch black down there, and it took me forever to find him. When I did, he was so hurt. I ..." She stopped for a moment to get control of the emotions that memory brought to her.

"Take your time, honey. Take your time."

"Thanks, Commander."

"Carla. Call me Carla. Go on with your story now."

"Okay, well, as I said, Jake was in bad shape when I found him. I gave him what weapons, food, and water I had, then went exploring for a safe spot. I found an old infirmary."

"Is that where you patched him up?"

"Yes. He'd passed out on me, so I stripped him off and did what I could."

"You actually did a pretty fair job. There's no doubt you saved his life there. Is that what happened, you both nurtured each other and that changed the connection between you?"

"Yeah, I guess. Look, I'll confess, I only had a couple of days, but he was mine for those days and I enjoyed it."

Carla smiled. "Tell me."

"Commander?"

"Carla, remember. Tell me what that was like for you."

"I don't know what kind of kicks you're getting out of this, but I'm done here." Angrily Twenty rose and strode from the office, ignoring Carla's pleas for her to return. She returned to her quarters, threw herself on the bed and wept. It wasn't long before a soft tap came on the door.

"Yes?"

"Twenty, it's Carla, please let me in."

"Go away."

"Please, Twenty. You didn't let me finish. We were just getting to the good part. Please let me in."

"Fine, come in, take your time, find a comfortable spot to kick me from. I deserve it. This is all my fault and I know it."

Twenty was shocked at what happened next. Carla stepped through the door, swiftly crossed the floor then pulled the confused woman into her arms. "I'm not here to kick you, and I'm not trying to torture you, Twenty. I'm trying to experience the magic of that time through your memories.

"I'm also trying to get a sense of what I have to do here."

"What you have to do?"

"Yes, that. Now, will you help me, please?"

"Commander?"

"Carla."

"Sure, Carla. I don't understand."

"Twenty, I swear I'll make it all clear to you before I leave this room. Will you help me?"

With a deep sigh Twenty nodded and stepped back out of Carla's arms. "Sure, just give me a hint at what you're trying to do."

"Okay, here, sit beside me and I'll explain. I was talking to Antha about our situation, you know, the three of us, you, me, and Jake. She told me that she used to be jealous that Morthel spent so much time with the crew of the Explorer, then she realized how much happier Morthel was. Antha decided to take joy in that.

"So, I'm trying to see if I can feel some of the sweetness you enjoyed in your time with Jake."

"Why?"

"Because the way things are now, you're tormented, Jake's way off his game, and so am I. I know you two are trying to stay away from each other, to make things go back to the way they were, for the greater good. It isn't working."

"I know. So what do you want me to do, kill myself? I tried that once; it didn't work."

Again Twenty found herself held gently in Carla's arms. "Oh gods no, girl, never that. That would just make things worse. No honey, the sad truth here is, things can't go back to the way they were, not ever again. That time is gone.

"No, now we have to find a way for all three of us to find a new happy place."

"New happy place?"

"Like Antha did. She realized there was no way for them to go back to the way things were on that colony. She had to find a way to be happy in the new world, this new time, she found herself in."

"And we have to do that?"

"We do."

"So. What's the answer?"

Carla chuckled. "I'm getting there, Miss Impatience. Work with me?"

"I can see it now, Carla."

"See what?"

"Jake said you can make him crazy sometimes. I can see how that works. All right, crazy woman, what do you want me to do?"

"Tell me about your feelings for Jake, when you realized what was happening, and that he returned your feelings."

"Are you sure about this?" Carla just nodded. "All right. I knew I was sinking, and that as soon as we were rescued it would be all over, I'd have to let him go. I could see it in his eyes sometimes and it gave me a thrill.

"The big thrill was the day the big lizard man came demanding I go with him. Jake stepped in front of me and told him I was his girl; that he would never give me up. I know he didn't realize what he'd said, but it gave me a thrill just the same.

"When they were gone Jake turned around and saw my face. He knew then and started to reach for me. I didn't dare let him touch me or it would be over, I'd never be able to let him go. Thankfully, Sessas got in the middle wanting a kiss on the noggin and broke the mood, but I did enjoy my title for a few hours before we were rescued."

"Your title?"

"Jake's girl."

"You liked the title. Want it back?"

"What? What are you saying?"

"Listen to me, Twenty, my sister. We've got a serious situation here, and it's causing trouble for the Reacher. Jake's miserable without you, I'm unhappy because a piece of him is always with you and because he's unhappy. You're special to the Admiral, and to Jake, and you're unhappy. The admiral and her lady companion are both losing far too much time worrying about all three of us, so they're unhappy, and all that is rolling downhill to the rest of the crew.

"Twenty, the Reacher can't function like this, it's endangering the entire crew and passengers."

"Did you just pull SUVI psychology on me?"

Carla gave a delighted little laugh. "Yes I did, did it work?"

"It did, you sure as hell have my attention now. So, what's the answer?"

Carla relaxed back and gave Twenty's hand a squeeze. "You already know the answer, girl. For you and Jake to be happy, you have to be together. For me to be happy I need to have my guy, happy, and beside me, a happy Jake makes a happy Carla. The trick here will be for me to enjoy you and to enjoy you with Jake."

"Okay, just a minute here, are you suggesting we become a threesome?"

"Yes. If you've got a better idea, I'm wide open to suggestions."

SUVI 20 sat back to gaze into Carla's eyes. "My god, you're serious, aren't you?"

"I am, girl. I've been racking my poor brain for days and I can't see any other way."

"But you don't have to do this, you've already got what you want."

"Maybe, but I don't have what I need. Yes, Jake still loves me, and he tries to show that every day, but there's a piece of him missing, you've got that piece, and I can't see any other way to get it back."

"Okay, and that's what we've been doing. You came in and held me, you've been sitting close to me to see if you can do it, to see if you and I could be close."

"Yeah, pretty much."

"So, how is this three way supposed to work? Do I get Monday, Wednesday, Friday, and you get Tuesday, Thursday, and Saturday with Jake getting a rest day on Sunday?"

Carla laughed heartily at that. "That's one way I guess, but I don't think it's the right one."

"Oh?"

"That still leaves you and me with the same problem, a man whose mind is only partly there with us and partly with the other one. No, girl, you and I are going to have to suck it up and learn to live together, share everything, all the time."

"My god, you're serious. Can you do that?"

"I have to, for the greater good."

Twenty got a naughty twinkle in her eye. "For the greater good, Carla? Are you saying you really don't like the idea?"

"I can adapt," replied Carla, as she pulled Twenty closer and kissed her. Twenty gave a soft moan and poured some enthusiasm into the kiss. Slowly, Carla released her. "See?" They were both breathing deeply and gazing into each other's eyes.

"Wow, Carla, I think you liked that."

"So did you."

"Yeah, okay, I'll admit it, I did. So what do we do now?"

"We have options."

"Oh goody, I like options," purred Twenty, as she pulled Carla closer and kissed her again.

"Mmm, Twenty, you have to stop that now."

"Why?"

"Because we can't do this alone, not the first time. If this is truly going to work, our first time has to be a full three-way first time."

"Carla, are you determined to do this?"

"Come on, you big SUVI, suck it up for the greater good."

With a naughty grin, Twenty rose to her feet. "All right, if I must then I'll do my best, for the greater good."

Carla smiled as she rose and hugged Twenty tightly. "We can do this, girl, we have to. There is no other answer, but you knew that all along, you just didn't think we mere humans could do it."

Twenty returned the hug. "I was afraid to dream, Carla. I knew I'd blown it big time, messed up your marriage, and was just trying to find a way to fade into the background until I disappeared. This whole thing is all my fault."

"Yes it is, and as your punishment you have to be mine and Jake's wife forever."

"I will, I swear I will."

"For the greater good?" grinned Carla.

"Hell no, for my own good. This is a great life; I screw up then I get the guy and the girl. It can't get any better than that."

With a laugh of delight, Carla took her hand and pulled her toward the door. "Come on, let's go tell Jake, scare him half to death."

"If he sees us coming holding hands he'll run for his life."

"Ah, he's tougher than that, he can take it. Come on Twenty, let's go find our guy."

THEY FOUND JAKE IN the mess, sitting with Jeannie, Amanda, Hal, and Lilly. Hal spotted them first. "Oh shit, Jake, run."

"What?"

"Carla and SUVI 20 just walked in holding hands."

"Oh shit, I'm doomed."

It was too late to run, they'd arrived, released their grip on each other then sat beside him, one on each side. "Hi guys, Carla, Twenty, what's up?"

"I got my title back, Jake."

"Your title?"

"Actually, it's a bigger title than she had before," grinned Carla.

"And that would be?"

"Well, for a while I was Jake's girl; that was my title." Twenty was grinning mischievously. "Now my title is Jake and Carla's girlfriend."

"Wait, what? What are you two trying to tell me here?"

"See, Carla, I told you it would scare him to death."

"Yeah, Twenty, I thought he was tougher than that. Look, Jake, I know this will be hard on you, but there's no other way, you have to suck it up and deal with it, for the greater good."

"All right, stop it now, both of you. Tell me straight up, what the hell is going on?"

Carla sighed and patted his hand. "Jake, Twenty's lost and hurting, you're lost without her, you still love me, but a piece of you will always be with Twenty, that makes you miserable, and that makes me miserable. Our friends spend all their time worrying about us.

"Since I'm so distracted, I'm not doing my job to the best of my abilities; neither are you, or the rest of our friends. The only answer is we move Twenty in with us."

"Seriously? My god, you're serious."

"I said the same thing," grinned Twenty.

Jake turned to her. "This is Carla's idea?"

"It is. How about it, big guy, two girls, twice the fun?"

"Twice the danger. Carla, are you... You are serious."

"Honey, I spent the day with Twenty. We talked our way around this a dozen times or more and we agree, this is the only answer."

"Yeah, well, it works great for me, I think, but what about you?"

"I'll manage."

"Carla?"

"Look, Jake, I can't see any other way out of this. I'll admit it wasn't my first choice, but I can't think of anything else. Every other option leaves somebody paying the price. Come on, buddy, let's show these SUVI we can tough it out for the greater good too."

"Carla, I ..."

"I know you didn't, she didn't either, but before start of shift tomorrow, we all will. Now, you go help Twenty carry her gear to our quarters."

He didn't move so she winked at Twenty. "Honey, take Jake and put him to work. Hey, and no hanky-panky without me, got it?"

"Got it, sweet sister. Come on, big guy, you get to carry the heavy stuff, I'll carry the hammer." She took Jake by the arm and pulled him to his feet. As they walked away Jake put his arm around Twenty's shoulders. Carla smiled softly.

"Carla?"

"Mandy, this has to happen, it does. If I start to come loose on this, you slap me and put me back on track. I have to be able to make this work."

"Carla, honey, ..."

"No, Mandy. These past weeks he was like he was back when he was still working in sanitation. If being with Twenty makes him happy then he needs to be with her."

"What about you?"

"I'm way better when he's happy, and I just spent the afternoon with her. The poor girl is tormented, and dammit, she got my maternal instincts going, then she got my hormones going. Maybe it's a SUVI thing, but I found myself needing for her to be happy too. I'll be okay, Mandy. Antha gave me the key."

"Antha?" asked Jeannie.

"Yeah, she said at first she wanted things to be like they were on the colony, but that could never happen. Morthel's a lot happier now than she was then. Antha chose to take joy in Morthel's new happiness. So, here's me, choosing to take joy from Jake and Twenty's new happiness. I get to love both of them, not such a bad deal."

Jeannie smiled at that. "No girl, it's not a bad bargain at all. Carla, I wish you all the happiness the universe has to offer. Go on now, or they'll start without you."

"They'd better not," she grinned, as she rose and fled the mess.

"Jeannie, what do you think?"

"I think Jake's in for an interesting life. Yes, sweetheart, I think they'll be just fine, and now we can stop worrying about them."

"Yeah, oddly enough, Carla looks better already. Hal, what do you think?"

"I think I'd better keep my mouth shut for my own good."

"Darn right you'd better," chuckled Lilly, as she lightly punched his arm, "and don't be getting any ideas."

Jeannie smiled and reached for Amanda's hand. "And on that note, I think we should return to the bridge and see if we're ready to set sail."

THE MIGHTY REACHER shuddered slightly then vanished from orbit around the planet of storms, hurtling at unimaginable speeds toward the binary star system that would be her next point of exploration.

Jake felt that familiar tremble in the deck and smiled as he carried the heavy container of Twenty's treasures towards the quarters he shared with Carla. Carla met them right at the door, and so did Linsey, Eighteen, and Sessas.

Sessas hugged Twenty tightly then turned a hard eye on Carla. "Whoa, girl," chuckled Twenty as she reached for Carla to pull her into the hug. "Easy, Sessas, Carla's my girl now too."

"Car ssa Ten tee frenss?"

"Yes, all friends now, honey." Twenty rose up on tip toe to kiss Carla on the top of the head.

Sessas gave a squeak of delight, hugged Carla, then Jake, then hurried to catch up with Linsey and Eighteen. "I think we just got the seal of approval," said Carla.

Jake nodded as he watched Sessas hurry away. "Yeah, I believe we did."

The End

NOTE FROM THE AUTHOR: This was the third story in a series of eight, I do hope you enjoyed it. Now for a peek at number four.

Chapter #1

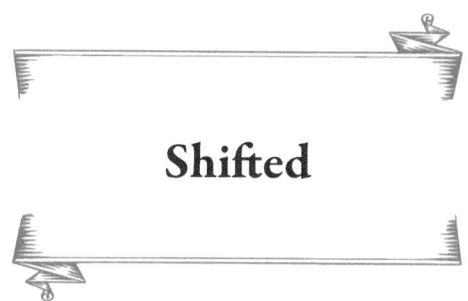

Shifted

The two armored combatants faced off again as the taller surged back to his feet. They circled each other, watching for an opening. Suddenly he feinted with his left then attacked from the right, but his smaller opponent had read the move. She ducked low and felled him with a leg sweep.

He landed hard on his back and groaned as he unstrapped his helmet and slowly stood up. She'd backed off and was signaling him to come at her again. The man tossed aside his helmet and began to unfasten the armor as he turned his back and walked away. "Hey, come on, we're not done."

"I'm done," he grumbled as he pulled off the armor then left without even glancing back at her.

Sheila Singh, Chief of Security, sighed, watching with mixed emotions while her lover left without another word. "Yes, I guess you are at that." She was reaching to remove her helmet when the ship suddenly lurched and spun, sending her flying.

THE MIGHTY STARSHIP, Reacher, began to slow her speed as she neared the binary star system that was her destination. Her passengers and crew, the last surviving humans in existence, gathered round the available view screens, anxious for the first look at the new system. As the ship dropped to sub-light speed she was suddenly rocked violently.

The ship bucked and spun about a few times, then was still. Her commander, Admiral Suvi-jean Sorenson began shouting orders as she picked herself up off the floor. "Damage report, all departments."

"Engineering here, Admiral," came the voice of Chief Engineer Moira Duncan. "We've got a hell of a mess, several injuries, but no hull breaches reported, and no atmo leaks."

"Medical here, Admiral, we've got a lot of injury reports coming in, but no deaths as yet. I'll have you some numbers as soon as we get it under control." With that Carla Marks, Chief of Medical, clicked off and went back to work.

Security Chief Sheila Singh was next. "Security here, Admiral. We'll work with medical to get things sorted out. More later."

Jeannie sighed and turned to her second officer who was rubbing his head. "Emmet, what the hell just happened? Where are we?"

"I have no idea at all, Admiral. I'll know more as soon as we get ..."

"Sensors back on line, Commander," came a voice from beneath a control panel.

"Well done, crewman. Where are we, Anita?" grinned Commander Jones, as he turned to sensors.

The woman at the sensor panel shook her head as she gazed at her screen. "I have no idea at all, Commander. We're supposed to be in a busy area of space, close to the binary stars, but we're well out in the deep dark. I can see a few faint stars and only one within easy reach. It's a single star, eight planets, perhaps two in the goldilocks zone."

Admiral Sorenson was right at her shoulder. "You're right, we're a long way from where we expected to be. Take your time, see if you can figure out where we are in relation to where we should be."

"Yes ma'am."

Jeannie smiled and turned back to Commander Emmet Jones, the man who was the heart and mind of bridge operations. "Emmet, are we at a full stop?"

"We are, Admiral."

"All right, hold us here for now, get the bridge back to top form; then see what you can learn of what happened, where we are, and what you think we should try next."

"Aye, Admiral."

Suvi-jean sighed and walked off the bridge, heading for her briefing room. She stopped in the corridor and checked in with each and every SUVI, making sure they, and Sessas, were all right. She then turned her attention to the Earalith. Jeannie finally arrived at the briefing room to find her lady companion, Captain Amanda Drake waiting for her.

"Jeannie, what happened? Are we okay?"

"I have no idea at all what happened, Mandy, but the Reacher seems to have survived. It'll take a bit of time for everybody to get things under control, then I'll call a full senior staff meeting, plus captains and passenger reps. The senior staff can bring us up to speed, then we'll see where we are from there."

"Where we are is halfway across the galaxy from where we started this morning, Admiral," said Commander Jones, as he limped through the door. "Thought I'd find you in here. Computer, display visual of known galaxy." A hologram of the slowly spinning galaxy appeared over the long table.

"Here's where we were, as we came out of hyper drive and went sub-light. Here's where we are now, just off the tip of this arm of the galaxy."

"Good gods, Emmet, are you saying we jumped from one arm of the galaxy to another?"

"Yes."

Jeannie gave a long slow whistle as she sat back in her chair and reached for Amanda's hand.

Amanda was gazing at the chart. "Commander Jones, can you tell me something. We poor humans believed ourselves to be alone in the universe until Jeannie showed us the Earalith colony. Since then, we've encountered a lot of evidence of other forms of life. Why is that; do you know?"

He smiled as he reached to point at the chart. "Well, Captain Drake, it seems that Earth is over here somewhere, a bit isolated. Even in the years we explored, we didn't get too far from home, galactically speaking.

"Now, the Earalithian empire was huge, and roughly over here where we finally brushed up against their territory at Elysium. Since then we moved in this direction, away from Earth and deeper into Earalith territory."

"And now we're way over here?"

"Apparently so. We must have passed through some kind of rift in space/time."

"Can we go back, Emmet?" asked Jeannie.

"I can't imagine how, Admiral. All our sensors tell us everything is normal out there in all directions. Whatever tossed us over here, left no sign of its existence."

"Well, if we can't go back, then we must then go forward. As soon as the ship is ready for travel, we'll proceed to that nearby star system Anita found."

He smiled and nodded. "I'll get everything organized on the bridge. We'll be ready whenever you are, Admiral." With that he saluted and limped out of the room.

Amanda sighed and sat back, still tightly gripping Jeannie's hand. "It's driving you nuts too, huh?"

"What?"

"The waiting, it's driving you nuts too. The toughest part of being the captain is telling the others what has to be done then waiting for them to do it."

Jeannie chuckled at that. "Yes, it makes me crazy. This being Admiral Sorenson has a few drawbacks, I'm itching to go do something, but I don't want to undermine the confidence of the people I've put in charge. What do I do now?"

"You've waited long enough, you can do walkabout now," said a voice behind her.

She turned to see her grandfather, Frank Baris, the former captain of the Reacher, smiling at her. "Grandfather?"

"I assume that as soon as the event happened, you were on the bridge issuing orders, contacting the various departments for reports, yes?"

"Yes."

"So, it's been a while now since we were tossed about, now you visit each department, get a report, express your confidence in your staff, look for other issues, then tell them to carry on and to keep you informed."

"Is that necessary?"

"Not actually, but it'll keep you from going crazy, and it'll let the crew and passengers relax a bit to see you being personally involved. Jeannie, they need to see you, a fully relaxed and confident you, moving about the ship.

"Amanda, you should be with your crew at your new ship as well."

"Is that where you're going, Grandfather? To your new ship?" asked Jeannie.

"Indeed so. I just thought I'd swing by here in case you were hiding out."

"Hiding out?"

Frank Baris smiled and sat down beside his granddaughter. "Jeannie, you've had your confidence shaken a few times lately, first when I got into trouble, and again when Jake got lost on the planet you named Stormy. Yes, Amanda and Linsey are amazing with their ships and crew, but this is the Reacher, your ship, your crew. You need to get out there and take command."

Jeannie reached over to lightly kiss his cheek. "You're right, Grandfather. Thanks for the pep talk."

"Just doing my job as your mentor." He smiled and patted her shoulder as he rose and walked out of the room.

Jeannie rose to her feet with a liquid grace. "He's right, Mandy, we've got work to do." Amanda smiled and gave her hand another squeeze, then fled the briefing room.

Also by Prudence MacLeod

Forgotten Worlds
Suvi
Echo of the Past
Survivors

Watch for more at https://www.prudencemacleod.com/.

About the Author

Jennifer Crandall writes and publishes under three different names, Prudence MacLeod, J.L.Crandall, and Jenni Leigh. Learn more about her on her website,

Read more at https://www.prudencemacleod.com/.

www.ingramcontent.com/pod-product-compliance
Lightning Source LLC
Chambersburg PA
CBHW020953180626
46814CB00003B/1069